The Fate of Felix Brand

Florence Finch Kelly

Illustrated by Edwin John Prittie

THE FATE OF
FELIX BRAND

By

Florence Finch Kelly

AUTHOR OF "WITH HOOPS OF STEEL," "THE DELAFIELD
AFFAIR," "RHODA OF THE UNDERGROUND," "EMERSON'S
WIFE, AND OTHER WESTERN STORIES," ETC.

ILLUSTRATED BY
EDWIN JOHN PRITTIE

1913

Mildred Annister made Apprehensive Inquiry about Him

CONTENTS

ILLUSTRATIONS

CHAPTER I

FELIX BRAND HAS A MYSTERIOUS EXPERIENCE

Felix Brand awoke with a start and looked about him with a puzzled stare. And yet there was nothing unfamiliar in what met his gaze. The bed wherein he lay and its luxurious appointments were of his own recent buying. He had himself designed the decorations of the room and selected its furnishings. As his eyes leaped from one object to another his bewildered glance seemed to slide unnotingly over the furniture, and the draperies, walls and pictures, indicative of a fastidious taste, that made up the interior of his bedroom.

But it was no more than a few seconds until his consciousness came again into accord with his surroundings. His look of perplexity quickly changed into one of satisfaction and amusement, and he exclaimed aloud:

"Good Lord, how vivid that was! Never before has it been so strong!" He rubbed his eyes, slapped his arms and moved about in the bed as if to be assured of his bodily intactness and smiled again as he thought:

"No, I'm here, all right, and I'm I, as usual! But it seems as if I'd only have to close my eyes to swing back into it again!"

His eyelids dropped as if in response to his thought, but quickly opened again, with a little frown, as he murmured, "No, I guess not. This is better!"

He rested his head upon his locked hands and stretched himself full length upon his back, as his eyes roved about the beautiful interior. They dwelt caressingly upon its details with the pride and pleasure of the creator and the satisfaction of the owner for whom possession has yet the bloom of newness.

It was a handsome face, framed in dark, waving hair, that thus lay back against the whiteness of the pillow; dark skinned, smooth shaven, squarish in its general outline, with regular, pleasing features; a mobile face, whose whole seeming would depend upon the expression by which it should be lighted. Just now it looked sensitive, amiable, satisfied, and, at the first glance, one would be sure that it bespoke a mind and soul of fine fibre. But if one looked a second time and more searchingly one would perceive some clouding and coarsening of that refinement, signs not yet marked enough to tell their story openly and not likely to be noted by the ordinary observer, but able to make the keener student of the human countenance doubt his first impressions.

"It's queer how much more vivid and real those dreams are nowadays—every time one comes it's stronger than ever it was before," Felix Brand's thought was running as he made ready for the day. The illusion that had possessed him as he awoke surged through him again and again with such force that it seemed almost strong enough to sweep his consciousness out of his actual surroundings. Razor in hand, ready to begin the task of shaving, a fresh onset, still more insistent, went whirling through his brain and sent a sudden numb sensation down his arm. He shook himself irritatedly.

"Confound it!" he muttered. "Can't I keep awake this morning? But I'm not sleepy—I'm as wide awake as ever I was! It's queer!"

He frowned at his reflection in the mirror, then suddenly his countenance glowed with interest. "I wonder if I could—I believe I'll try!" he exclaimed aloud. "Jove! What an experience it would be! It's worth trying!"

He turned to lay the razor down and felt his eyes fasten themselves in a devouring stare upon its bright blade. An instant, and he was startled by the sound of a strange voice which he caught just as it was dying out of his ears, a strong, vigorous voice, speaking in tones of authority.

"Who's that?" he cried out, glancing about the room in surprise. What he had heard had sounded like a name and his thought snatched at it as it faded quickly away from him. "Hugh Gordon!" he repeated softly, and said it over to himself as he gazed dazedly about the room. Well might he turn the name over and over in his mind and wonder about it, for it was destined to become to him the most hateful thing in the world.

"Nonsense! What's the matter with me this morning?" and he shrugged impatiently. "I don't know anybody named 'Hugh Gordon' and there's nobody in here anyway. The sound must have come from the hall, or, maybe, from the street."

His eyes fell upon the clock and he started with surprise. "Why, it can't be that late! Only a moment ago I looked and it was—I couldn't have seen straight or something's gone wrong with it. Anyway, I'd better get a move on."

He turned briskly to the mirror to resume the operation of shaving and stared again as he put out his hand to pick up the razor. For it was not where he had laid it down a moment before. His wondering glance quickly discovered it on the other side of the dressing table, and bewildered amazement overspread his countenance. It was laden with the results of recent use.

"The devil!" he gasped. "I hadn't shaved! I hadn't even lathered!"

But the half fearful look of inquiry he darted into the mirror showed his face to be freshly shaven, and in the usual manner, except the upper lip, where had been left the faint, dark stubble of a mustache.

CHAPTER II

"LIKE OTTAR OF ROSES OUT OF AN OTTER"

"Breakfast is a little late, Harry. Delia is in one of her introspective moods and it has made her slow. I hope you won't miss your boat!"

She turned an anxious face toward her sister, who was entering the room, and Henrietta Marne smiled reassuringly, as she set down a suitcase, laid her hat and coat upon a chair, and replied in a hearty, cheerful tone:

"No, indeed! I've plenty of time. And I was glad to have an extra five minutes with mother. Do you think she's better than she was yesterday? Bella, I'm afraid I ought not to go to Mr. Brand's theatre party tonight!" And her countenance clouded with anxiety as they seated themselves at the breakfast table.

"Don't think of missing it, Harry! Mother will be all right. She seems a lot better this morning."

"Y-e-s, I thought so, but I'm afraid she'll miss me tonight. It always seems to please her when I come home in the evening."

"Of course, dear, we'll both miss you! You're the man of our household, you know, and you go out and battle with the world every day and bring us a fresh breath from it every night!"

"And you always 'meet me with a smile,'" laughed Henrietta.

"Of course! And we'll be twice as glad to see you tomorrow night, and we'll smile twice as big a smile, because you'll have such a lot of things to tell us."

"Mr. Brand has a curious effect upon me that I don't quite like." Henrietta frowned thoughtfully into her coffee cup while she hesitated, as if choosing words for further speech. In shirtwaist, linen collar and cloth skirt she looked trim, well groomed, alert. Fair-haired and fresh-colored, her expression capable, composed and sweet-natured, she was what a Scotchman would call "a bonny lass."

Her sister, also fair, was smaller of mold and daintier of look and manner. She appeared a little older, but her features were finer and more regular and a twinkle of humor barely hid itself in the corner of her blue eye, as if ready to spring forth at the first encouragement.

"This begins to sound romantic!" chaffed Isabella. "Let's hope he's at least a pirate in disguise."

"No, let's not. Because then he'd sail away and I'd have to hunt a new job. And it is such a nice place, Bella! I don't believe another girl in my whole class just fell into such good luck as I did. He seems pleased with my work, too."

"I know he is, Harry, because Mrs. Annister told me last week that Mr. Brand thinks he has found a jewel of a secretary—the best he's ever had. I was waiting"—and a gleam of mirth sparkled in her eyes as she smiled fondly upon her sister—"to tell you until some day when you'd be feeling blue. But I just couldn't wait any longer."

Henrietta flushed with pleasure. "I'm so glad to know that! If he'll just keep on being satisfied a few months longer, we'll have this place paid for!"

"Oh, we're going to pull through all right!" Isabella exclaimed, hopeful conviction in her tones and smile. Then she puckered her brows and did her best to look doubtful and alarmed as she went on in a tragic half whisper, her blue eyes dancing: "If he doesn't turn pirate and sail away in the meantime, or, maybe, make a villain out of you, with this wicked influence you're getting alarmed about, so that you'll maybe steal your own salary and run away with it and leave mother and me to star-r-ve! To think that a famous architect should be just oozing badness all around him like that—as Mark Twain said, 'like ottar of roses out of an otter'—at the same time that he's evolving such beautiful things out of his brain! Ugh! It's awful!"

Henrietta laughed, a short, chuckling laugh that suggested deeper amusement than it expressed. "Is there anything you wouldn't make fun of, Bella? Very likely it isn't he, after all, but just my own innate wickedness coming to the surface. It's only that I feel a great desire to amuse myself, and am more willing to be selfish about it than I used to be. Three months ago I wouldn't have gone to this theatre party, with mother ill and you alone with her. I know I'm a beast to do it, but I do want to go dreadfully, and——"

"And you're going, and you're not to coddle your conscience any more about it. It's all right, and we're all right, and mother and I would feel we were two beasts if you stayed away on our account. What makes you think Mr. Brand responsible for this awful depravity? Because he invited you to his house-warming?"

"Oh, no! It was thoughtful and lovely of him to include poor little me among his guests, and I'm as grateful as—Cinderella. But he sometimes says some little thing, in connection with what we are doing, about the pleasure there is in beautiful things and how it and the joy one ought to get out of life enlarge and deepen one's existence. And then I begin to feel, away down inside of me, a longing for pleasure, and as if I could reach out and grasp all sorts of—of things, just for my own enjoyment."

"And that makes you feel dreadfully wicked!" Isabella's laugh tinkled through the room, a lighter, merrier sound than her sister's. "Dear me! As if we didn't all feel that way once in a while!"

"You never do," Henrietta interrupted.

"Don't inquire too deeply into my feelings, unless you want to be shocked. Suppose we have some hot toast to cheer us up after this awful confession. Delia," to the maid who entered in response to her ring, "have you some fresh toast ready?"

"The toast is awfully good this morning, Delia," said Henrietta smiling at her. "It's always nice, but it's particularly good, exactly right, this morning."

"Thank you, Harry!" said Isabella as the maid disappeared. "I'm so glad you said it. Maybe it will make her feel better. Did you see that determined, dare-and-die look on her face? I'm sure something's going to happen!"

"And we've raised her wages twice already," the other exclaimed, as her face took on the same anxious expression that had just clouded her sister's.

"Yes, and we can't pay her any more than we're giving her now. She isn't worth it and we couldn't afford it if she were."

"Just as we've begun to feel sure she was satisfied and would stay. Oh, Bella! It's too bad! But maybe it's no worse than it was the last time we got scared, when her cousin was married and she wanted a day off. You remember, she had two days of the introspective mood then."

"Thank you, Delia! It's done to a turn!" and Isabella smiled sweetly at the returning maid, who retreated a step and stood still, fumbling her tray, an embarrassed, determined look upon her face.

"It's perfectly lovely," chimed in Henrietta with enthusiasm.

The girl shuffled from one foot to the other but her expression did not relax. Isabella cast an "I-told-you-so" look at her sister and glanced expectantly at the maid.

"What is it, Delia?"

"I'm thinkin', Miss Marne, you'd better be lookin' for a new girl."

"Why, what's the matter? You don't want to leave us, do you?"

"No, miss, I don't want to, an' that's the truth. But I don't think I'll be stayin' any longer than you can get another girl."

"What's the trouble, Delia?"

"It's lonesomeness, Miss Marne. It's that respectable out here that there's niver a policeman comes along this street for days at a time. An' the milkman comes around that early I niver see him, an' anyway he's elderly an' the father of four. An' it's so high-toned, there ain't a livery stable anywhere, an' so there's none of them boys to pass a word with once in a while. An' there's only the postman, an' him small and married."

There was silence for a moment while the maid shuffled her feet and turned her tray about and the sisters bit their lips. Then Isabella exclaimed, in a tone of brisk sympathy:

"Yes, Delia, I understand how you feel, and I don't blame you at all, but——"

"Don't make up your mind right away, Delia," Henrietta broke in. "Think about it a little longer. Maybe something will happen."

"And only think, Harry," Isabella groaned, as Delia left the room, "what a wonderful bargain that real estate agent made us think we were getting, just because there were so many restrictions there could never be anything or anybody objectionable within a mile of us!"

"I had an inspiration just in the nick of time," Henrietta replied. "Mrs. Fenlow told me, when she was in the office the other day, waiting for Mr. Brand, that she is going to move her garage to this end of her property, which you know is just a block away, with an entrance from this street—she hoped it wouldn't annoy us—and she said she was going to have a new chauffeur. And we can hope, Bella, that he'll be young and tall and handsome and inclined to be flirtatious with good-looking maids who sometimes work in front door-yards nearby. Why, here's Billikins! You naughty doggie, where have you been?"

A white fox terrier had bounded into the room and was giving her exuberant greeting, having stopped first to drop at her feet a rag-doll that he carried in his mouth. "There, that will do," she laughed as he sprang to her lap, and thence to her shoulder and testified his overflowing affection with voice and tongue. "Get down now and take care of your babykins!"

"I must go now," she declared, and, rising, began putting on hat and coat. "I'll just run upstairs and kiss mother good-bye again. If anything should happen, Bella, or should you want me to come home for any reason, you can 'phone me at the office until five o'clock, and after that at Dr. Annister's. Mrs. Annister, you know, is going' to chaperon Mildred and me. Wasn't it sweet of her to ask me to stay all night with them!"

Five minutes later she came hurrying downstairs again, and Isabella, waiting for her at the front door, put the suitcase into her hand, pressed an arm about her waist, and gave her a farewell greeting.

"Have just as good a time as you can, Harry, dear," she said gaily, "so you'll have all the more to tell mother and me tomorrow night!"

The morning sun shone down through the golden autumn foliage of the maple trees that lined the street, and now irradiated Henrietta's figure and then dyed it somberly as she passed with rapid step through open space and shadow. Isabella watched her progress down the quiet road toward the avenue, half a dozen blocks away, whence came the clang of street cars and the rattle of traffic. But the girl turned now and then and cast an eager glance in the other direction.

"I'm so glad she could go tonight," Isabella was thinking. "She works so hard and she doesn't have many pleasures—neither do I! But I don't mind—very much!" She cast another glance up the street and caught sight of a smallish man's figure bending one-sidedly under a burden of other people's joys and sorrows as he passed in and out of the gateways in the next block. A pleased smile brightened her face and she turned back to watch her sister's progress.

"There! She was just in time to catch that car! She's just a brick, Harry is! What a funny notion about Felix Brand! If it was little Bella, now—" She threw up her head saucily and danced a step or two as she faced about to see how near the postman had come.

"'An' him small an' married!'" she repeated to herself and laughed softly as she watched his slight, burdened figure on its slow progress. "Poor Delia! If I was in her place I'm afraid I'd flirt with him anyway!"

She ran down the walk to the gate and greeted him with a merrily smiling, "Good morning."

"Only one this morning, Miss Marne," he said, smiling back at her, and then added, as he saw her face brighten, "but it's the one you want, I guess!"

"Yes," she gaily replied, "you're always very welcome when you bring me a letter like this!"

She was keenly conscious of the caress in her hand as she held the letter in close clasp. Once inside the door again, she pressed the missive softly to her cheek as she whispered, "Dear Warren! You dear boy! I just knew you were writing to me yesterday, and you didn't disappoint me!"

CHAPTER III

THE MASK OF HIS COUNTENANCE

It was a curious mixture of people whom Felix Brand had bidden to the theatre party and house-warming with which he celebrated the setting up of his bachelor household gods in a studio apartment house. But the varied contents of that mixture were not so much indicative of catholic tastes in human nature as of an underlying trait of his own character, a trait which led him to look first, in whatever he did, for his own advantage. But whatever their differing attitudes toward life there were few of his guests who did not follow his movements with admiring eyes and think of him as one of Fortune's favorites.

For in this artistically decorated and luxuriously furnished apartment there was nothing to hint that until recent years he had lived as yoke-fellow with severest economy. The son of a school-teacher in a Pennsylvania town, the family purse had had all that it could do to provide for him a course in college and the training for his profession. But at the beginning of his career he had won a rich prize in an architectural competition, and afterwards commissions and rewards and honors had flowed in upon him in constantly increasing measure. While he did not yet quite merit the adjective which Isabella Marne had applied to him, there was every promise that he would soon be, in truth, a "famous architect."

Although he had barely entered his third decade, certain characteristic features of his work had already won attention, and these had been praised so much, and had begun to exercise so evident an influence, that many looked upon him as destined to be and as, indeed, already becoming, the leader of a new and fruitful movement in American architecture. A Felix Brand design, whether for a dwelling, a church, a business building, or a civic monument, was sure to be marked by simplicity of conception, exquisite sense of proportion and rhythmic harmony of line.

"What a perfectly charming manner he has!" said Miss Ardeen Andrews to Henrietta Marne, who knew of her as a rising young actress. "And such wonderful eyes! Why, there is a caress in them if he only looks at you!"

"Yes," replied Henrietta in a matter-of-fact way, "it's a very pleasant expression, isn't it? But it doesn't mean anything in particular. It's just their natural expression."

"And he's not only handsome," Miss Andrews went on with enthusiasm, "but he's the most sensitive and refined-looking man I've met in a long time." And she flashed a glance of covert admiration across the room at their host, who was talking with two men of such different type as to make his own courtly manner and intellectual features noticeable by contrast.

A little later Henrietta, passing the two men, heard them speculating, in tones touched with an Irish brogue, as to whether or not the young architect was already making money enough out of his profession to pay for such surroundings as these in which he was settling himself.

"There's money enough in it when you get to the top," one of them was saying. Henrietta remembered him as a certain district political leader, Flaherty by name, with whom her employer had lately held several conferences. "Money enough to buy old masters to paper your walls with and velvet chairs to sit in for a year, and never the same one twice. But Brand's not up to the top yet. He must have some other jug to go to, and I'd like to know just what it is and how big it is!"

Henrietta could have told them what it was, and she was presently reminded of it when two men were presented to her and she recognized their names as that of the firm of brokers through which Felix Brand had for some time been carrying on what she knew to be very profitable operations in stocks.

"The doctor won't forget us entirely, will he, Mrs. Annister?" the host was saying to the tall and handsome woman with iron-gray hair and warm-colored cheeks who sat beside him at the supper table.

"I hope not; but you know I never vouch for him. Mildred impressed it upon him that he must be here in time for supper," and she glanced at the young replica of herself at Brand's other hand.

"Yes," confirmed the girl, "he promised very faithfully that he'd come as soon as he could. But he was to see a case tonight in which he's very much interested, and if he gets to thinking and reading about that, you know, Mr. Brand, that he is just as likely as not to forget all about us."

"Oh, yes, that case!" said her mother. "It's most curious and interesting—one of the sort that makes you feel creepy."

"Do tell us about it then," exclaimed Ardeen Andrews, farther down the table.

"It's a man possessed by the illusion that his dreams are the real thing and his waking hours are imaginary. Just think what a topsy-turvy state that must keep his family in!"

Felix Brand looked up with sudden interest, but before he could speak a man's voice called out from the other end of the table, "The doctor doesn't consider faith in one's dreams evidence of a pathological state, does he, Mrs. Annister?" It was Robert Moreton, a young author, whose name was of frequent occurrence in magazine tables of contents.

"If he does," Mrs. Moreton broke in, "how crazy he would think you, Rob! You see, when he is writing a story," and she glanced up and down the table, "Robert imagines it's being acted out around him, and I have to be the heroine and the villainess and the parlor maid and the cook and answer to all their names."

"That must give some variety to existence, Mrs. Moreton," said Brand. "And variety is the best spice for life that I know of."

"Do you know that story of Colonel Higginson's," Moreton went on, "called 'A Monarch of Dreams,' about a man who developed the power of controlling his dreams and became so delighted and absorbed in them that he gave himself up to the life he lived while asleep and allowed his real existence to wither away until it was of no consequence at all to him or any one else? It has always seemed to me a wonderful bit of eerie imagination. And there are such alluring suggestions for experiment in it!"

Felix Brand's brown eyes were fixed in a speculative stare upon the mass of roses that glowed at the center of the table. Miss Marne, glancing at him, knew that, whether or not he was thinking of them, he was conscious of their beauty in every fibre of his being. "I wonder," he said slowly, and she saw Mildred Annister's gaze turn quickly upon him as the girl bent forward with parted lips. "I wonder very, very much," he repeated, "just how much one could do toward making one's dream-people come alive. I mean, toward making the different kind of person one sometimes is in a dream the real person when one is awake. You know how different you seem sometimes when you are asleep, not at all the same kind of person you are when you are awake. Now, wouldn't it be interesting if you could make yourself be that person sometimes after you wake up? It seems to me it would be a delightful change from being the same person all the time. This being tied fast to yourself year in and year out gets very monotonous."

Miss Annister gave a little gasp and leaned nearer to him, distress in her eyes.

"Don't say that!" she begged, hardly above a whisper. "Don't even think such things! You are you, and I wouldn't have you different for worlds and worlds!"

Her disturbed little appeal was shielded from observation by a vivacious feminine voice which called out simultaneously: "Please finish my house before you turn yourself into anybody else, Mr. Brand! You know we've only settled on the back porch and one dormer window, so far, and I'll leave it to these good people if that's enough for a family of six to live in!"

Henrietta smiled discreetly at her plate, for she knew along what a tortuous path of inchoate ideas and breezy caprices Mrs. Grahame Fenlow, upon the sightliness of whose new chauffeur she and her sister were basing their hopes of keeping their maid of all work, had led the architect in his attempt to design a new house for her.

"Aren't you afraid, mother," exclaimed Mark Fenlow, from his seat beside Henrietta, "if you don't decide pretty soon whether you want that dormer window in the cellar or the roof and whether the back porch is to be before or behind the house, that Mr. Brand will be driven to try a new personality, or incarnation, or—or drink, or whatever you call it!"

"Why, here's the doctor at last," cried Felix Brand as he rose to greet the newcomer and lead him to his seat at the table.

Dr. Philip Annister, smiling affably at the company, scarcely looked the famous specialist in nerve diseases that he was. Short and slight in physique, his head, when he stood beside his handsome wife, was barely on a level with hers. Wherefore, his shoes, ever since his wedding day, had been noticeably high of heel, and rarely was he known to wear other head covering than a silk hat. He had cast aside the look of abstraction which commonly possessed his thin, pale countenance and his manner and speech of modest geniality soon won for him the favor of all the heterogeneous company to whom he was not already known. His wife noticed that his eyes rested frequently upon their host and later she said to him:

"Felix is looking handsomer than ever tonight, isn't he!"

"Yes, I suppose so," he answered hesitatingly. "But, Margaret, there's an expression growing on his face that I don't like. It's creating a doubt about him in my mind."

"What do you mean? His manner tonight toward all this queer mixture of people has been perfect—cordial, unassuming, delicately courteous and friendly toward every one. And, really, Philip, I don't know a handsomer man! His face is so refined, and those brown, caressing eyes of his are enough to turn any girl's head. I don't wonder in the least that Mildred is so completely in love with him. What is it you don't like about his looks, Philip?"

"I don't quite know, and perhaps it isn't fair to him to put it into words until I do know. It is less evident tonight, when he is all animation and his thoughts are full of the entertainment of his guests, than I have seen it sometimes lately. You know, Margaret,

Felix has an unusually expressive countenance. It's like a crystal mask, and it's bound to reveal the very shape and color of his soul. I think I begin to see signs in it of selfishness and grossness—"

"Oh, Philip! How can you! Grossness! He's the most refined——"

"You haven't announced Mildred's engagement yet, have you?" her husband interrupted. "I'm glad of that," he went on in a relieved tone as she shook her head, "and I hope you will not for some time."

"Mildred is beginning to look forward rather eagerly to being married," said Mrs. Annister, smiling soberly. "I'm almost afraid she's more in love than he is."

"I'm so glad I came tonight. It has been lovely!" Henrietta Marne at that moment was saying to her host, at the other side of the room.

"You have enjoyed it?" and he bent upon her his brown eyes with their look of caressing indulgence. "I'm glad of that, for I'm afraid you don't have as many enjoyments as a girl ought to have, by right of her youth and beauty and charm."

"I was afraid I ought not to come, because my mother is ill."

"Ah, that Puritan conscience of yours, Miss Marne! Don't be so afraid of it when the question is nothing more than getting some innocent pleasure out of life."

"But one isn't afraid of one's conscience. One just takes counsel of it, or with it."

"Of course! But if one—you, for instance—yielded to it more than its due—and it really is insatiable, you know, if you let it get the upper hand—what a wretched affair life would be! Simply unendurable!"

"But there's always a satisfaction in doing what one ought to do, Mr. Brand—don't you think so?—even if it is hard."

"Oh, if you like your satisfaction to taste hard and bitter! I don't! I think it's much better to hold ourselves free to take advantage of all the possibilities of happiness, little and big, that come our way. It's really a duty that we owe ourselves. And, of course, if we are happy

16

we make others about us happy too. You, I'm sure, need enjoyment so much that it would be a great mistake for you to throw away any opportunity. And I'm very glad you didn't neglect this little one!"

Mrs. Fenlow and her son were at his elbow to say goodnight, and as he shook hands with Mark, whose mother had already passed on to an exchange of confidences concerning hairdressers with Miss Ardeen Andrews, he laid his hand affectionately on the young man's shoulder and said in a low tone:

"You're coming tomorrow night, Mark, of course?"

"Sure! D. V. and d. p.—God willing and the devil permitting!"

"It will be very different from this," and Brand smiled slightly, a winning, deprecating smile, as with the least perceptible motion of his head he indicated the company that filled his spacious drawing room. "But a man doesn't want his relaxations to be all alike, any more than he wants all flowers to be of the same color."

CHAPTER IV

BILLIKINS IS FRIGHTENED

It was inevitable that the personality of Felix Brand should loom large in the home of his secretary. Mrs. Marne was a semi-invalid and suffered frequent relapses into more serious illness. The care of her and the management of their little household were Isabella's part, and to these two, much confined at home and by necessity cut off from nearly all outside pleasures and interests, the chief daily event was Henrietta's return from her busy hours and responsible tasks in the architect's office. But, of still more importance, their worldly welfare hung upon the salary which he paid to the younger sister.

Mrs. Marne's husband had been a physician in one of the smaller cities of Massachusetts; but, though a New Englander, he had not possessed the characteristic thrift of the sons of that region, and consequently his widow and his daughters found, after his death, that the settlement of his affairs left them a very slender sum of money. It was necessary that one of the young women should become an income earner, and it was decided that Henrietta, since she had a better head for affairs and more liking for business, should take this share of their burden. There was enough money to give her a course in secretarial training in a women's vocational college in Boston and to support them all in economical comfort until she should be ready to begin her work. As she was at once successful in finding a position in New York, they invested the few hundred dollars still left in a first payment upon a little home in Staten Island, and they were now carefully husbanding Henrietta's salary and paying off the remaining debt upon the instalment plan.

It was through Dr. Annister that Henrietta found a good position so quickly. He and Dr. Marne had been classmates and warm friends during the years of their medical training, and afterward, although one had gone to New York and become one of the famous specialists of his generation and the other had sunk into the obscurity of general practice in a small city, they had kept up their friendship in a desultory way, with occasional meetings at medical conventions and now and then a letter. When Dr. Marne died, a missive came from his friend that seemed so simple and genuine in its feeling that it deeply touched Henrietta, to whom fell the duty of answering it, because of her mother's stricken condition.

The memory of that letter and a warmly reverent feeling for the friendship that had called it forth stayed long in her heart. And at last, when she was ready to try conclusions with the world, and felt sure, with the usual conviction of youth, that it would be much better to go somewhere else to begin, she wrote to Dr. Annister, telling him briefly her plans and hopes and what her training had been. And the famous Dr. Philip Annister interested himself in the daughter of his old friend, and at once found for her a well-paid position as secretary for Felix Brand, his prospective son-in-law. Mrs. Annister also showed much kindly feeling for the girl and often had her stay overnight at their home for a visit to the theatre or the opera.

Between Mildred Annister and Henrietta there existed a friendship which made up in outward warmth what it lacked in depth. For Mildred, with her woman's heart but lately awakened and filled to the brim with absorbed and adoring first love, could not help some secret resentment that any other woman should be anything to her beloved or give him any service. Her good sense told her that this was unreasonable, while her respect and kindly feeling for Henrietta made her ashamed of it. So she did her best to conceal it and in the effort overdid her expressions of affection. Henrietta would have responded to these with girlish ardor, for she liked Mildred and greatly admired her tall and stately beauty, had she not felt some barrier just below the surface that kept her as reserved, in all the little confidences that usually go on between young women, as was Mildred herself. She did not even know of the semi-engagement, to which Dr. and Mrs. Annister had not yet given their full assent, that existed between Mildred and Felix Brand, although she felt sure that the girl was whole-heartedly in love with him.

As the weeks went on and autumn merged into winter, Henrietta sometimes noticed a harried look upon her employer's countenance. She wondered much about this, for he was winning success and honors in ample measure. An international committee of artists and architects, sitting in judgment upon the competitive designs submitted for a memorial building to one of the country's heroes, had announced their decision awarding the prize to Felix Brand. He had been made a member of the municipal art advisory commission and a little later a national society of architects had elected him to its presidency. There were private commissions in plenty, enough to keep him and his assistants busy. And, finally,—and Brand laughingly told his secretary that he considered this the most signal success of his career—Mrs. Fenlow had approved his last design for the country house she purposed to build up the Hudson and had been moved to transports of enthusiasm over its every detail.

In addition to these honors and successes, Henrietta knew that he was making much money outside of his profession; that his operations in stocks were nearly always profitable, that once or twice they had been richly so, and that he had bought a large number of shares in a marble quarry for whose product his designs often called.

So she marveled much within herself that he should so often look careworn and show a furtive anxiety in his eyes and face when he had, or was rapidly winning, almost every good thing that mortals count a source of happiness and when even her intimacy with his affairs did not reveal a solitary cause for distress or uneasiness of mind.

She spoke of this sometimes at home. For her mother and sister were always concerned to know what her day had been, and Felix Brand being so important a person to their lives, they were deeply interested in whatever he did or said and in everything Henrietta could tell them about him. They were scrupulously careful not to ask or to speak about anything that would approach too nearly her confidential relations with her employer. But outside those lines there was a large and interesting territory wherein they could and did have much converse together about the architect, his success, and his personality.

On a bright and mild Sunday morning in mid-winter, whose sunshine was full of that guileful promise of spring with which the tricky weather goddess of the Manhattan region loves to play pranks upon its residents, the two Marne sisters, in their mother's room, were chatting with her as she reclined in the sun beside a south window.

"I've some good news," said Henrietta. "I didn't tell you last night, because I knew we'd all be gossiping in here this morning and it would be so cosy to talk it all over then. Mr. Brand has raised my salary, to date from the first of this month!"

Mrs. Marne's thin hand sought her daughter's where it lay upon the arm of her chair and then hastened to wipe away a tear or two. For she was nervously much broken and her tears, whether of joy or sorrow, came easily.

Isabella sprang up, exclaiming, "Harry! How splendid!" And the two girls hugged each other delightedly and kissed first each other and then their mother. Then they kissed each other again and whirled about in a waltz measure. Billikins, the white fox terrier, quickly put a stop to this exuberance by endeavoring to take part in it himself, barking furiously and making ecstatic rushes between them.

"The second time, dear!" exclaimed Isabella as they settled down again, cheeks flushed and eyes shining. "Only think of it! At Christmas, and now again so soon!"

"It isn't so very much," said Henrietta, "only ten dollars a month more, but it will be a lot for us, and it means a great big lot to me, because it makes me feel that I'm succeeding. What is it, Billikins? Do you want to come up? And you've brought babykins, haven't you? Come on, then, both of you." The fox terrier was begging and wriggling beside her, his inseparable companion and plaything, a dilapidated rag-doll, in his mouth. She lifted them to her lap, where, after much licking and nuzzling of the doll, he curled himself up to sleep.

"Of course you're succeeding!" cried Isabella. "How could you help it when you're the cleverest girl in New York and work the hardest and—have such a nice home to stay in at night!"

"It will soon be nicer," rejoined Henrietta with a laugh, "when we get rid of its mortgage decoration. Now we can get that all paid off by the end of the summer and then we'll be sure of a home, whatever happens."

Mrs. Marne pressed her hand in a closer clasp. "Dear child! You and Bella are the best children a mother ever had. I've just been thinking that I really have three children, a son as well as two daughters. For you're just as good as a son, Harry, besides being a daughter too. When you were born, dear, I was disappointed that you weren't a boy, and sorry for you that you weren't."

"Were you sorry about me, too?" demanded Isabella saucily.

"You, dear! Why, when you came—you were the first, you know—I was too proud and delighted to think of anything but just that I had you. By the time Harry arrived I had learned more about what it means to be a woman and I was sorry I had brought another into the world. But I soon got over all that and was so glad to have you both. After all, girls, it is a grand thing to be a wife and a mother!"

"Yes, if you can only get your salary raised often enough," said Isabella gaily. "And I guess," she went on as she saw a little wave of amusement cross her mother's face, "I'd better have that settled right away. I'll write to Warren that I shall expect an increase every time Harry gets one. Tell us more about your raise, Harry. What did Mr. Brand say?"

"Oh, he was very nice—but he always is nice, just as kind and courteous as can be. He said he was much pleased with the good judgment and the care with which I had managed things while he was away. Before this, when he's been gone for a day or two or three, he has made some arrangements beforehand and has told me where he would be so that I could telegraph or 'phone him on the long distance if necessary. But lately he's been called away twice so suddenly that he left me no directions and I didn't know his address, and so, although he was gone only two or three days each time, I had a good deal of responsibility. But he was very kind and praised everything I did and yesterday he told me that he thought I deserved a reward and as he might be called away again the same way, he didn't think it was fair to put so much more upon me without paying me for it."

"Isn't he lovely!" exclaimed Isabella. "As Delia says about Mrs. Fenlow's chauffeur, 'he's sure very gentlemanly and strong!'"

"Indeed, you've been most fortunate in getting so good a position, Harry, dear!" said Mrs. Marne, her voice trembling with her depth of feeling. "I fairly ached with anxiety over your going into this secretarial work, but Mr. Brand has proved to be all that even his secretary's mother could expect or wish."

"And here he is, right now!" cried Isabella as she glanced from the window at the sound of an automobile in the quiet street. "And if he isn't going to honor our humble but happy home with a call from his very handsome self!" she went on excitedly as the machine slowed down and its occupant, glancing at the house numbers, stopped in front of their cottage.

He told Henrietta that he had just learned it might be necessary for him to leave town that day and that he wanted to give her some instructions for her guidance if he should be away more than a day or two. His manner was disturbed and restless, although not lacking in its usual suave and gentle courtesy, and she noted in his face, more strongly marked than she had seen it before, that troubled, anxious look concerning which she had already wondered much. And from the whole man there seemed to her to emanate an unconscious appeal, as of one in such sore and badgering straits that he knew not where to turn for help.

"I may be able," he said, "to—put off this trip, to make some arrangement about—this matter, so that it will not be necessary for me to go. I hope so—I don't want to leave the office just now. And, by the way, if I do go, there's another thing. If there should be a letter in my general mail—not marked 'personal,' you know—" he hesitated, and Henrietta observed that he turned his eyes away and did not meet her gaze as he went on, "but not of the regular business sort, just glance at the signature first thing, won't you, please? And if it should be signed 'Hugh Gordon,' don't read it, but lay it aside for me to look at when I return."

He straightened up and she could feel the effort of will with which he conquered his perturbation and continued in a more offhand way:

"Gordon is apt to write confidential things about his own affairs and he is the sort of man who would never think of marking a letter 'personal.'"

Billikins trotted into the room, his doll in his mouth, and, laying his burden down in mid-floor, as if to make easier the concentration of his faculties upon the duty of investigating this stranger, advanced with signs of ready friendship. Brand responded to his overtures, but the dog, after a preliminary smell or two, broke into a sudden howl and trembled as if with fear. Reproved by Henrietta, he hastened back to his babykins, with which he rushed to a place of safety beneath her chair. There she heard him giving vent to his emotions in subdued whining and growling and in much worrying and tearing of the rag-doll.

Brand rose to go, but lingered beside his chair and made conversation, as though loath to take his leave; and Henrietta, catching a glimpse of Isabella passing through the hall, called her in.

Whenever Isabella entered a room it was like the advent of a merry little breeze. For all the look and manner of her suggested buoyant spirits and gaiety of heart, from the lurking twinkle in her blue eye to her light quick step. Daintiness and prettiness characterized her attire, which she carried gracefully, to the accompaniment of a soft, faint rustle. With pleasure Henrietta watched her employer's face brighten and clear as he talked with her sister. The agitation faded from his manner and presently she was aware that the impression she had had of struggle and appeal, which had begun to tense her own nerves, had disappeared.

"I don't wonder," she thought. "Bella is so light-hearted and so merry, and so pretty and sweet, too, that she could charm away anybody's dumps. I wish I had some of her gift that way—I'm always so serious."

Brand suggested that they should take a spin with him in his automobile. "The day is so fine," he pleaded, as they hesitated a little before answering. "You don't know how splendid it is! And the roads are good down through the island." He glanced from one to the other and Henrietta saw in his brown eyes a look of eager wistfulness.

"It would be lovely and a great treat for us," she said. "You've no idea, Mr. Brand, what a temptation it is. But we don't like to leave mother alone, for she's never very well."

"Oh, is that all?" he exclaimed. "Then bring her along! It would do her a lot of good. Wrap her up well and I'll carry her out to the auto."

He begged Isabella not to desert him while Henrietta went to prepare their mother for the drive.

"How well they get on together," said Mrs. Marne, smiling at the gay laughter that now and then floated up the stairs.

As they came slowly down, the elder woman leaning heavily upon the other's shoulder, Felix Brand ran into the hall, exclaiming:

"Why didn't you call me and let me bring her down!" And at once, notwithstanding her assurance that she could walk, he picked her up and carried her to the street in his arms, saying, "I can just as well save you that fatigue," and carefully settled her in the automobile.

"You'll sit in the front with me and help me drive, won't you?" he said to Isabella as the two girls came out cloaked and furred.

"Yes, do, Bella," said Henrietta cordially in response to a glance from her sister, "and give me a chance to show what good care I can take of mother."

Although Isabella was the elder of the two by three years and formerly had been accustomed to take the lead between them, since the younger had become the support of the family she was beginning, quite unconsciously, to lean upon and defer to her sister. During the drive Henrietta and her mother exchanged many pleased glances as they listened to the merry chatter and the frequent laughter that drifted back from the front seat. It was a smiling Felix Brand, suave, serene, and courtly of manner, who helped them from the machine on their return and carried Mrs. Marne into the house.

"Please don't," he said as they protested their enjoyment of the ride and their sense of his kindness. "For I assure you it has meant a great deal more pleasure and benefit to me than it possibly could to you."

"I think he really meant that," said Henrietta when the three women, alone again, were talking over what Mrs. Marne called their "little escapade," "because when he came he seemed so disturbed and depressed and by the time we got back he was quite himself again. I think it was mainly you, Isabella," she smiled at her sister, "for you seemed to have a very stimulating effect on him."

"Oh, I'm willing to be a cocktail for him whenever he wants to bring his auto over here. Never mind, mother," and she kissed one finger at Mrs. Marne in response to that lady's shocked "Isabella!" "That's just modern symbolism, you know. And the ride has made you look as if you'd had one yourself. I'm going to write to Warren that I've found a much nicer and handsomer man than he is and if he doesn't get a stronger grip on my heart right quick it's likely to get away from him."

"Bella, dear! Don't say such things!" admonished her mother in a grieved tone.

Isabella flew to her side and patted her cheek and kissed her brow. "There, there, mother! Don't you know I'm just funning? Warren is the best man in the world, even if he hasn't got bee-youtiful, caressing brown eyes, and I love him awfully, and we're going to be married and live happily forever after. But, all the same, Felix Brand is perfectly lovely, and you think so too, now, don't you, mother dear!"

"We all think alike about Mr. Brand, I'm sure," she answered.

"Except Billikins," amended Henrietta, and then told them of the fox terrier's disgraceful behavior. "It seemed so queer for him to act that way," she added, "when he's always so friendly toward visitors and so effusive that he usually has to be put out of the room."

"It was strange," said Mrs. Marne, "for with his pleasant voice and gentle manner you would think Mr. Brand would be as attractive to animals as he certainly is to people. And he must be as kind and

26

sweet-natured as he seems, for not one young man in a thousand would have taken the trouble he did to give three forlorn women a little pleasure."

Henrietta made no reply as she laughed with her mother at the lively scolding Isabella was giving to the dog, but her thoughts were busy with the problem of why Felix Brand had seemed so anxious for them to go with him.

Her loyalty to her employer would not let her throw the least shade upon their enthusiastic appreciation of his courtesy and kindness. But her months of work at his side—she had been his secretary almost a year—had given her an intimate knowledge of his character and of his habits of thought and feeling.

She had learned that his habitual mental attitude was, "What is there in this for me?" He did not indeed use just those words or give such crude expression to his self-centeredness; but she had come to know that personal advantage was the usual mainspring of his actions. Presently deciding that Isabella's enlivening effect upon his mood had inspired his desire for their company, her mind went on to busy itself with speculation over the cause for his despondency and uneasiness.

"I believe it must have something to do with that Hugh Gordon he mentioned, whoever he is," she thought. "For he seemed most disturbed when speaking of him. Maybe it's some relative who is giving him trouble—some black sheep of his family, very likely."

She walked to the window and stood there silently, her thoughts hovering around this unknown personality, and became conscious of the upspringing in her breast of a feeling of disapproval and even of enmity toward the man because of the trouble he seemed to be giving to the employer she admired so much and for whose appreciation and unvarying kindness she felt so much gratitude.

Then there surged over her a wave of discontent, against whose threatened onslaught she had half consciously been doing battle ever since she had talked with Felix Brand in the morning. Now it was upon her. How monotonous seemed her life, how destitute of the pleasures that most girls had as their right! If she could only use for her own enjoyment some of that money she worked so hard to earn! But that everlasting mortgage on their home which had to be paid off—how the thought of it irked and galled when she longed to travel, buy beautiful clothes, go to the theatre and the opera, have young friends and ride and drive and play golf and dance and sing with them. It was the playtime of life and she was having to spend it in work, work, work!

"Oh, there isn't anybody who would enjoy all those things as I should," she thought, "and I want them so!"

She turned impatiently from the window and her glance fell upon her mother, smiling gently and happily as she lay back in her easy chair, and remorse entered her heart.

"What an ungrateful little beast I am," she stormed at herself, "to feel like that when I ought to be thankful I can earn money enough to keep mother in comfort! Was it because Mr. Brand was here that I felt that way? Harry Marne, be ashamed of yourself! Aren't you old enough to be responsible for your own thoughts?"

She sat down beside her mother and taking her hand pressed it tenderly against her cheek.

CHAPTER V

MRS. BRAND'S DREAM SON

It was half a week after that spring-like Sunday when Felix Brand motored to his secretary's home on Staten Island, and a feathery pall, white as forgiven sins, was sifting down from the heavens upon all the eastern seaboard. In a town within the suburban radius of Philadelphia its mantle of purity lay almost undisturbed upon lawns and streets and vacant lots. Two women were looking out upon the snow-covered earth and snow-filled sky from the side window of a cottage near the edge of the town. One, small and gray-haired, perhaps looked older than she was because of the pathetic droop of her shoulders and the worn, patient expression of her face. But lined and sad though her countenance was, it told of a sweet and gentle soul and it was lighted now with a look of pleasure.

"Just look at it, Penelope!" she exclaimed, a little thrill of enthusiasm in her voice. "I never saw it snow harder, or look prettier! Isn't it beautiful!"

She turned a pair of soft brown eyes upon a younger woman sitting beside her in a wheel chair, who put down the book she had been reading, and sighed as she answered: "Yes, it is beautiful, mother, very beautiful. But when I look at it I can't help thinking how long it will be until spring comes again and I can be out in the yard under the trees."

The mother put out her hand, small and once of the shape that chirognomists call "the artistic hand," but now wrinkled, bony and toil-hardened, and rested it gently for a moment upon the mass of dark, waving hair, already well-threaded with gray, that crowned the other's head. Her face filled with sympathy but her voice broke cheerfully upon the silence:

"Oh, it won't be long now, Penelope, and not a bit longer because of this beautiful storm!"

The figure in the wheel chair bent forward again and looked out upon the pearly whiteness of the earth. It was a sad travesty of the human form, undersized, humped and crooked. But it bore a noble head with a broad, full brow and a strong, intellectual face that had in it something of the elder woman's sweetness of expression. But in her brown eyes the other's softness and wistfulness gave place to a keener, more flashing look that told of a high and soaring spirit. And in the lines of her face was a hint of possible storminess, though it was softened by an expression of self-mastery, eloquent of many an inner battle waged and won.

The window from which they looked commanded one side of their own wide yard, a vacant block, and beyond that a cross-street. The snow was feathering down so fast that it gave to the air a milky translucence through which bulked dimly an occasional traveler on the other thoroughfare. Penelope's eyes fixed themselves upon one of these vague shapes.

"Look, mother!" she exclaimed. "Do you see that man just turning the corner to come this way? It looks like Felix!"

"So it does!" the other cried.

They were both silent for a moment as they gazed intently at the dim figure, gaining definiteness now with each step toward them. "It doesn't walk like him," Penelope commented, her face already showing that she knew it was not he. But the mother hung a little longer to her hope. "No, it isn't Felix," she presently acquiesced, disappointment evident in her gentle tones. "I so hoped it was, at first."

With a firm, rapid stride the young man was coming eagerly up the street, his eyes upon their house. "He doesn't walk at all like Felix," Penelope repeated thoughtfully as his figure became more plainly visible through the veiling snow, "but it's curious how much like him he looks, after all."

"See, Penelope!" the mother exclaimed, reaching out to grasp her daughter's hand in sudden enthusiasm. "See how he comes out of the snow mist! Isn't it just like a figure in a dream getting plainer and clearer, and more like life!"

Penelope pressed her mother's hand and smiled up at her fondly. "Just like you, mother, to make something pretty out of a disappointment!"

They gazed at the advancing figure with renewed interest and saw that the man, with slightly slackened pace, seemed to be closely observing their house and yard. What he saw was a one-story red cottage, needing paint, its green window shutters looking old and somewhat dilapidated, its yard, of ample size and dotted with trees and shrubbery, surrounded by a wooden fence in whose palings were occasional breaks and patches. It was a commonplace object in an ordinary winter scene, but he seemed to feel in it the deepest interest. There was even a frown on his brow as his alert glance rested on a broken pane in the kitchen window.

"It has been a long time since Felix was here—six months, hasn't it, mother?" said Penelope, leaning back wearily again as the stranger passed from her range of vision.

"Hardly so long as that, dear. It was last fall. But, of course, he is very busy. He hasn't the time to travel around now and go visiting, even over here to see us, that he used to have, before he had begun to be so successful. We mustn't expect too much." As she spoke, her gentle tones as full of indulgence and excuse as her words, she moved to the front window and sought the figure of the stranger, now striding along the snow-covered sidewalk in front of her own yard.

"Penelope! He's coming here!" she exclaimed, starting back and dropping the muslin curtain she had pushed aside. "He's turning in at our gate! He does look like Felix—a little. Who can it be!"

Penelope bent forward to peer through the curtains and saw the man mounting the steps to their little veranda and stamping the snow from his feet. Instantly she wheeled her chair about and sped it into the adjoining room as her mother opened the door to their visitor.

"You are Mrs. Brand, I think? Felix Brand's mother?" he said. "I am a friend of his—my name is Hugh Gordon—and as I was coming to Philadelphia I promised him I would run out here and see you."

As they entered the living room his keen, dark eyes swept it alertly, as they had the exterior of the house. A shade of disappointment crossed his face.

"Your daughter?" he asked abruptly. "May I not see her, too?"

Mrs. Brand hesitated. The shyness of her girlhood years still lingered in her manner when in the presence of strangers, and she glanced at her visitor, then at the floor, and her hands fluttered about her lap. Gordon's face and eyes softened as he looked at her. There was something very sweet and appealing in the gentle diffidence of this little, plain, elderly woman.

"Penelope doesn't often see people—anyone, and she is very unwilling to meet strangers. Perhaps Felix told you—you know——"

"Yes, I know. I understand how she feels, but I want very much to see her. I know Felix well, and I know a good deal about her, enough to make me honor and admire her very much. Won't you tell her, please, that I came out here particularly to see you and her, and that I shall be much disappointed if I have to go back without meeting both of you?"

Penelope soon returned with her mother and both had many questions to ask concerning Felix. Was he well? Was he working harder than he ought? Was his new apartment very beautiful? Had Mr. Gordon seen the plans for the new monument with which he had won in the national competition?

He used to send them photographs, Penelope said, but lately they knew little about his work unless they saw pictures of it in the newspapers.

But, indeed, they didn't expect so much attention from him now, her mother quickly added, for as his work increased and became of so much importance they understood how necessary it was for him to give it all his time and thought.

"It would really be selfish," she went on, "as I sometimes tell Penelope, to want him to spend time on us, writing long letters, or coming over here, when we know that his success depends upon his devoting all his energies to his work."

Penelope, silent and gazing out of the window, was conscious of Gordon's quick glance at her, and was conscious too of the appeal in her mother's wistful brown eyes, which she felt were turned upon her. So many years these two had passed in intimate companionship and in loving ministration on one side and utter dependence on the other, that spoken word was scarcely needed between them to make known the mood of each to the other.

In immediate response she turned, with a smile that lighted up her controlled, intellectual face, and said:

"Of course, we quite understand how occupied Felix is all the time, but that doesn't keep us from liking to know about him. So your visit, Mr. Gordon, is quite a godsend, and you mustn't be surprised that we ask you so many questions about Felix and want to know all about him and what he is doing."

Her voice was low, with rich notes in it, and her manner quite without self-consciousness. Notwithstanding her deformity and her secluded life, she betrayed neither shyness nor embarrassment. In both manner and speech was the poise that is usually the result of much association with the world.

"Yes," Gordon was assenting, "Felix has many irons in the fire, and he is planning to have more. But he thinks of you both, and you would be surprised to learn how much I know of you—through him." He rose and as he moved across the room to Penelope's chair he continued: "You, I know, Miss Brand, love the sunshine and the out-of-doors." He hesitated a moment and then went on, pouring out his words with a sort of abrupt eagerness:

"But I don't want to call you 'Miss Brand!' It doesn't seem as if I were talking to you. I feel as if I had known you so long that I want to call you 'Penelope,' as Felix does. Will you let me? You won't mind if I do? Oh, thank you! You are very kind to me, for I realize what a stranger I must seem to you, although I feel as if I had known you both such a long time. Well, then, Penelope," and he smiled and nodded at her, as he crossed the room to the front window and drew back the curtain, "how would you like to have one end of this porch enclosed with glass, so that you could sit out there with your wraps on, all winter, even on days like this, and feel almost as if you were out of doors? It wouldn't seem quite so shut in as the house, would it?"

She leaned back with a sigh and then smiled. "Yes, it would be pleasant. But it is now some years since I quit wishing for the things I can't have."

"Ah, but you're going to have this," he exclaimed, his face beaming. "Felix is preparing a little surprise for you, but he gave me permission to tell you about it."

The expression upon the faces of both women and their little exclamations told Gordon, as he glanced from one to the other, that their surprise was as great as their pleasure.

"Felix is going to have it done for you," he went on, "as soon as he returns. I forgot to tell you, and perhaps, as he went away rather unexpectedly, he didn't write you, that he was called out of the city a few days ago on pressing business. I saw him when he was leaving and I know you may expect to hear from him about the porch as soon as he returns. I'll tell him how pleased you are about it."

They gave him messages of gratitude and love and the three of them discussed the little improvement with the intimacy of old friends. Several books, one of them still open at the page where Penelope had been reading, were on a table beside the window. Gordon took them up one by one and ran over their titles. "Ah, poetry—and fiction—and biography—how catholic your interests are, Penelope! But I knew that already. Sociology, too. Yes, I knew that is your favorite study. It is mine, too, but I haven't had as much time yet to read along that line as I would like. What have you lately read on that subject?"

She told him of some of the recent books that had interested her most and mentioned the titles of others that she thought would be worth while.

"After you read them," he said, in his quick, decisive way, "I'd like very much to know what you think of them."

"I'd be glad to talk them over with you, but it's not likely I can have the opportunity of reading them very soon. I take books from the town library, and so many people always want the new ones that sometimes my turn is a long time coming."

He was making a note of their titles. "I'll tell Felix you're interested in them," he rejoined casually, "and I'm sure he'll send them to you."

Wonderment filled the minds of both mother and daughter and showed in their faces.

"You and my brother must be great friends," Penelope hastened to say, "although you seem to be so different from him. You resemble him a little—yes, a good deal, physically, but in manner, expression and, I should think, in mind and temperament and character, you must be very different. But perhaps that only makes you the better friends. You see," she went on, smiling frankly, "mother and I are already talking with you as if we knew you as well as Felix does."

"I hope that you will, and that very soon," he responded, and his manner reminded her for a fleeting instant of the winning deference, the slightly ceremonious politeness, of her brother's habitual demeanor.

"That was just a little like Felix," she thought. "Perhaps he has been with Felix so much that he has unconsciously caught something of his manner. Felix has a very pleasing manner, but—I like this man's better."

"I don't think Mr. Gordon so very unlike Felix," her mother was saying, "that is, unlike Felix used to be. Naturally, he has changed a good deal of late years. It's to be expected that a young man will change as he grows up and enters upon his life's work. But Mr.

35

Gordon looks more as I used to think Felix would when he grew up, and something as my husband did when we were married, but still more—" she paused, searching his countenance with puzzled eyes. He started a little, as if pulling himself together.

"Now I know," she exclaimed. "Penelope, Mr. Gordon looks like your Grandfather Brand! If you wore your hair longer, Mr. Gordon, and had no mustache, you'd look very like an old picture I have of him when he was young. He was such a good man and I admired and respected him so much! I used to hope, when Felix was a little boy, that he would grow up to be like his grandfather."

"He has grown up to be a very able man," Gordon responded gravely. "He has opened the way toward being a famous one, and he has the capacity to go far in it. He has much more talent than I."

"Are you an architect, too?" asked Mrs. Brand.

"No, I have not done anything, yet. But it is only now becoming possible for me to do anything of consequence." His manner and expression grew suddenly even more earnest and serious. "And there is so much that I want to do, that needs to be done, so much that urges one to action, if he feels his responsibility toward others."

Mrs. Brand was looking at him with startled, swimming eyes. "Oh, you are so like Father Brand!" she exclaimed. "How often have I heard him speak in just that way! He was rather a stern man, because he wanted to hold people to a high standard. But he fairly burned to do good in the world and make it better. I used to hope, when Felix was a little boy, that he'd have the same kind of spirit when he became a man."

She stopped and her worn face flushed at the thought that she had almost spoken slightingly of her son, had at least hinted disappointment in him. She fidgeted with embarrassment as silence fell upon them and she felt Gordon's eyes upon her. She could not resist his steady gaze, and as her eyes met his the look in them stirred her mother-heart to its depths and set her to trembling. She saw in it wistfulness and loneliness and felt behind it the persistent heart-hunger of the grown man for the mother in woman, for maternal understanding and solicitude and affection.

"I knew right away," she said afterward to Penelope, "that he'd never known a mother's love and that he was homesick for it and it made my heart warm toward him more than ever. He looks so young, even younger than Felix, and that minute he seemed as if he were just a boy."

"I hope you will let me come again," said Gordon as he bade them good-bye. He took Mrs. Brand's toil-worn hand in both of his and with gravely earnest face looked down into hers as he went on: "And if you should hear—if I should do anything that seems—well, not friendly, toward Felix, I hope you will try to believe that I am not doing it to injure him, but because it seems to me right and because I truly think it for his good."

Mrs. Brand was still trembling and she felt strangely moved. But her usual shyness was all gone and she did not even notice that she was finding it easy to talk with this stranger, easier, indeed, than it had been, of late years, to talk with Felix. Her heart swelled and throbbed with yearning over him.

"I am quite sure," she said, "that you will not do anything unless you are convinced that it is right and for the best. No matter how it may seem to others, I shall know that you expect good to come of it."

"Thank you!" His voice was low and it shook a little. He bent over her hand and raised it to his lips. "If I had a mother I should want her to be just like you! Will you try to think of me, sometimes, no matter what I do, as being moved, perhaps, by the same spirit, at least the same kind of spirit, as that of—of Felix's and Penelope's grandfather?"

Her patient face and her brown eyes glowed with the emotions that thrilled and fluttered in her heart. Belief in him, the sudden, sweet intimacy into which their brief acquaintance had flowered, his seeming need of her, and her own ardent wish to respond with all her mother-wealth, filled her breast with new, strange life and stirred her imagination.

"I shall think of you," she answered with sweet earnestness, "as if you were the boy—a man—I don't know how to say just what I mean, but perhaps you'll understand—as if you were the man who had grown up out of the dreams I used to have about my boy.

"Don't think," she added hastily, "that I'm displeased or dissatisfied with Felix, because I'm not, though what I've said might give that impression. He is a good son and I am proud and glad to be his mother. But a mother has so many dreams about a son when he is little that no boy could possibly fulfill all of them. He must follow his own bent, and the other things she has dreamed for him must be left behind. So I'll just feel as if, in some mysterious way, those dreams had come alive in you. And—oh, Penelope! Do you remember what I said a little while ago, when we saw Mr. Gordon coming toward us out of the storm, that it was just like someone taking form and shape in a dream? I'll think of you as my dream son, Mr. Gordon—Hugh!"

Impulsively he seized her hand again and held it closely clasped in both of his. "Will you do that? Will you think of me in that way?"

Penelope, in her wheel chair beside them, fidgeted her weak, misshapen body. Her nerves were tense with an excitement which she knew was not all due merely to an unexpected call from a stranger. Unaccustomed emotions, strong but undefined, were filling her breast and tugging at her heart. To her sharpened perception it seemed almost as if something uncanny were hovering in the room. She shivered and leaned back wearily. What spell was coming over them? Were those two beside her, strangers until an hour ago, about to sink sobbing into each other's arms? And was she, Penelope, the calm and self-mastered, about to shriek hysterically?

"How ghostly you two are becoming," she exclaimed, with an effort at vivacity, "with your dreams and your spirits! You make me afraid that Mr. Gordon, substantial as he looks, will melt away into thin air before our very eyes!"

"We are getting wrought up, aren't we?" Gordon assented as he turned to her. "And you are pale, Penelope! I hope I haven't tired you too much. Seeing you both, and your being so kind, have meant a lot to me, more than you can guess. And if your mother is going to be my dream mother, Penelope, you'll be my dream sister, won't you?"

He smiled as he said this, then all three laughed a little, more to lessen the tension which all of them felt than because they were amused, and presently the two women were alone again. Afterward, as they talked over all the incidents of the afternoon, they recalled that it was the only time during his long call that Gordon had laughed, and they wondered that a young man who seemed so full of vigor and life should have so serious a demeanor.

CHAPTER VI

WHO IS HUGH GORDON?

Felix Brand did not appear at his office the next day after his call at the home of his secretary, and she inferred that he had gone on the journey of which he had spoken. The week went by and he did not return. It was longer than any previous absence had been, but Henrietta, being prepared for it, was able to keep his affairs in order. Nevertheless, as the days slipped by and no message came from him, she began to feel solicitous. On Monday and Tuesday of the next week, Mildred Annister made apprehensive inquiry concerning him over the telephone. On Wednesday, big headlines in all the newspapers told a city not yet so cynical but that it could read the news with surprise, that Felix Brand, its successful and promising young architect, was charged with having won his appointment upon the municipal art commission by means of bribery.

An investigating committee had been secretly feeling about in another city department with no thought of uncovering corruption, or even of looking for it, in a body of city servants whose character, occupations and ideals lifted them so far above suspicion.

Then they received an intimation that even there all was not as pure as it might be and had called before them the man from whom the hint had come. Guided by his information they had followed a devious trail, apparently quite clean at first, but showing undoubted befoulment as they neared its source. And finally they had traced it to its beginnings in an unsavory local politician, Flaherty by name, who was powerful in his own district and therefore had influence in his party organization. And Flaherty, they had discovered, had been well rewarded for efficient work in engineering the matter and inspiring those above him to suggest and secure the appointment.

Scarcely had Henrietta reached her office on the morning of this publication when Mildred Annister rushed in, anxious, excited and indignant.

"Harry, dear, have you heard from him? Do you know where he is? I know he would write to me, if he could write at all, before he would to any one else, but, oh, do tell me if you know whether anything has happened to him!"

"No, Mildred, dear, I don't suppose I know much, if any, more than you do. But certainly nothing serious could have happened or some message would have been sent here."

"You're not keeping anything from me?" the girl demanded, staring at Henrietta with wild, suspicious eyes. "Oh, Harry, you don't know what all this means to me! I've hardly slept for the last two nights! You must tell me everything! Oh, I know you are his confidential secretary and you must not betray his trust, but— you don't know—I've never told you—I'm almost the same as his wife. We're engaged, and we'd have been married before this but for some notion father has. So I've the right to know, Harry—you must tell me all you can!"

Henrietta bent toward the girl sympathetically. "I don't think you need to be so anxious," she said reassuringly, although her own heart misgave her. "I'm so glad to know about your happiness," she went on, stroking Mildred's clenched hand where it lay upon her desk, "and I'm sure this will come out all right. He went away very suddenly. Did—did you know that he was going?"

Mildred nodded and wiped some hysterical tears from her eyes. It was a moment before she could control her voice: "Yes. He had promised to come to our house on Sunday evening. But instead he sent me a note—the dearest little letter—" and her hand involuntarily moved to her breast as she paused and smiled. Her listener marveled at the light that played over her countenance for a moment. "He said he had been suddenly called out of the city and might be away several days, but would see me again as soon as he could get back, and in the meantime I must not be anxious. But I can't help it, Harry! I'm wild with anxiety! Oh, if anything should happen to him I couldn't bear it—I couldn't live!"

"Harry, Dear, Have You Heard From Him!"

"There, there, dear, don't be so alarmed. Calm yourself and I'll tell you all I know." Mildred was hysterically weeping and Henrietta moved to her side and with an arm about her shoulders soothed her and went on:

"Sunday morning he motored over to my house to tell me that he might have to be out of the city for a few days and to give me some directions about matters here in case he should have to go. He said he didn't know how long he would be gone but hoped he would be back inside of a week."

"Sunday—then you saw him after I did. Did he seem well? Was he all right?"

"Yes, except that he looked anxious and disturbed."

"Oh, I knew there was something wrong! Why didn't he come to me and tell me all about it! I would have comforted him! I'd have done anything for him—I'd have gone at once and been married, whatever father might say, if he had wanted me to!"

"I don't think it could have been anything very serious, dear, nothing more than just a temporary depression of spirits, because— well, you know what a merry little piece my sister is and how she jokes and laughs and says nonsensical things until you can't help being cheered up and laughing, too. She seemed to amuse Mr. Brand and he was very kind and took us all for a ride in his auto. And, oh, Mildred, you should have seen how lovely he was with my poor, frail mother! He insisted that she must go, that it would do her good, and he carried her in his arms out to the auto and back, and was as tender and careful with her as a son could have been!"

"How like him!" the girl beamed. "He is so good and kind! Harry, there isn't another man like him in this whole world! It would kill me to lose him!"

"We had a delightful ride and Mr. Brand seemed to enjoy Bella's merry talk. She sat with him, and when we came back and he returned to the city he was looking quite himself again."

"Oh!" said Mildred, drawing back and looking at Henrietta with narrowing eyes. She was too absorbed in her own intense emotions to perceive the embarrassment which suddenly gripped her companion. Henrietta, wildly groping about in her own mind for something to say which would relieve the momentary strain, chanced upon what her employer had said about Hugh Gordon and her own subsequent suspicions, which had been made sharper by the charges in the morning newspapers.

"Mildred, dear!" she exclaimed. "Has Mr. Brand ever said anything to you about a man called Hugh Gordon?"

"Hugh Gordon!" The girl straightened up, her color rising and her eyes flashing with indignation. "Why, he's that dreadful creature who is responsible for all that horrid mess in the papers this morning, isn't he?"

"The committee's report says that he gave them their first information and told them how to get the rest of it."

"Horrid creature! I know it's all a mess of lies! No, I never heard of him before. Why do you ask? Do you know anything about him? Did Felix ever speak of him to you?"

"Only once—last Sunday," Henrietta hesitated.

"What was it?" the other demanded. "What did he say? Oh, I knew you were keeping something from me! Tell me, Harry!"

"Truly, dear, it wasn't anything of any consequence. It wasn't about himself, or his business, so I suppose it's all right for me to tell you. He only asked me, if any letters should come signed 'Hugh Gordon,' not to read them but to put them aside for him when he should return, because this man was likely to write confidentially about his own affairs. That's all Mr. Brand ever said to me about him—the only time he's ever mentioned the man's name. But I thought maybe—it was just my own conjecture, you know—that maybe this Gordon is some dissipated relative, some black sheep of his family, whom Mr. Brand is trying to help."

"Oh, I see through it all! It's as plain as day!" cried Mildred impetuously. "This Gordon is a blackmailer who is trying to force money from Felix! I knew all the time there wasn't a word of truth in that disgusting story! Felix has been helping him—perhaps he's a cousin, or something, and he has demanded more and more money, and Felix has refused, and now in revenge he has done this! And he's got Felix shut up somewhere to make him give in! That's why I haven't heard from him! Oh, it's perfectly plain! The thing to do now is to find this horrible Hugh Gordon and make him tell where Felix is!"

The office boy entered to say that some reporters wanted to see Mr. Brand's secretary. Henrietta was about to send back the message that as she knew nothing whatever of any consequence it was not worth while for her to see them, when Miss Annister interposed.

"No, Harry, let them come in," she said. "Perhaps they will know something that we don't."

While the reporters questioned Henrietta they stole many a covert glance at Mildred Annister, who sat beside her, dignified and beautiful, her cheeks glowing and eyes brilliant with excitement, listening with intense interest.

Henrietta soon told them the little that she knew about the matter. Mildred waited until they had asked all the questions they could think of and then, leaning forward in her absorption and gazing intently at one of the group, she said: "Now tell us all that you know about this Hugh Gordon. I want to know all you can tell me, because I have a theory about him."

Her intensity and eagerness roused the hope that perhaps here they might find something with which to embellish a story in which, so far, they had uncovered little to add to that of yesterday. But first they must know who this lovely girl was.

"You are a relative of Mr. Brand?" one of them hazarded.

"I am Mildred Annister, Dr. Philip Annister's daughter, and I am Felix Brand's promised wife."

The instant ripple of interest among the reporters caused Mildred to shrink back in sudden self-consciousness, her face scarlet.

"But please don't put that in the papers," she went on. "It's of no interest to anybody but us, and we don't want the engagement announced yet. I told you so you would understand how much right I have to be interested. I am perfectly sure this dreadful creature, Hugh Gordon, is at the bottom of the whole business, that these charges in the papers this morning are nothing but revenge for his failure to blackmail Mr. Brand, and it is just as certain as can be that he has got Mr. Brand imprisoned somewhere, maybe drugged, and the thing for you to do now is to find this Gordon and make him tell where Felix is. Oh, please do!" she ended, with a sudden drop in her manner, her voice choking.

Seasoned news gatherers though they were they could not repress all sign of the gratification they felt at her words. They loosed a battery of questions upon the two young women, but soon discovered upon what a slender basis Miss Annister had based her theory.

They could tell her nothing whatever about the mysterious Hugh Gordon. But they promised to follow her clue and to hunt him down if he could be found. They went away well pleased, for even if this suggestion should not lead to anything of consequence they had enough already to warrant "scare heads" over tomorrow's story and to furnish a narrative of even more "human interest" than the one set forth that morning.

Mildred Annister opened the paper the next morning with the greatest eagerness and expectation. But she sank back in horrified dismay as she saw the headlines. "I told them they mustn't say anything about me or our engagement," she said to her father, "and now just look at that!"

"Well, well," he replied, as he glanced over the article, "they've been fairly decent, at any rate, in the way they've written it up, though it's not pleasant for you to be thrown into the limelight like this. As for their making known your engagement, it can't be helped now, so there's no use worrying about it. But you mustn't want to be married too soon, daughter."

Mildred welcomed this final grudging half-acquiescence and felt that it was well worth the price. "Now it will be easy to persuade him to let us be married soon, when Felix comes back," she thought.

But the morning's news had not an atom more of information concerning the architect's whereabouts than she had known the day before. Hugh Gordon also had disappeared. Before the publication of the investigating committee's report several newspaper men had seen him and talked with him about it, but the next day they could not find him anywhere, nor any one who had the least idea whither he had gone. One member of the committee knew Brand very well and, in pursuit of Miss Annister's idea that Gordon and the missing architect might be relatives, the reporters had questioned him about Gordon's disappearance.

There was some resemblance, he said, although he had not thought about it at the time. Gordon was a larger man, he thought, and a younger, and his manner was very different. Brand was always affable, very polite, and inclined to be somewhat ceremonious; but Gordon was brusque, rather aggressive, and seemed to be much in earnest. His evident sincerity and honesty had impressed the committee very much. But, on the whole, he concluded, there was some resemblance between the two men in feature and coloring; enough, perhaps, to indicate that they might be relatives.

Mildred was keenly disappointed to find so little of consequence or of promise in the news of the morning, but the committeeman's description of Brand's accuser confirmed her in her conviction.

"If they can only find him," she thought, "it will solve the whole mystery and set Felix right before the public again."

She telephoned to the paper which had seemed most active in the hunt for Gordon, begged that they would continue the search, and made the city editor promise to call her up if they should find out anything new about him or come upon any trace of his movements. For the rest of the day she refused to leave the house and sat all the time in high-strung expectation near the telephone, that she might not lose a moment in responding to its ring. But no call came until late in the evening, when the city editor rang her up to say that his men had discovered absolutely nothing new, and that nobody had any more idea what had become of either Brand or Gordon than they had had the day before.

CHAPTER VII

FELIX BRAND READS A LETTER

When Henrietta Marne entered her office on the morning of the second day after the publication of the charges against Felix Brand, she found her employer already there, but sitting moodily at his desk, his head in his hands.

As she came forward, exclaiming joyfully and making anxious inquiries about his welfare, he shrank back for a bare instant, with a slight turning away, as of one who fears observation. But he quickly recovered himself, rose with his usual deferential politeness and gave her cordial greeting. She noted that he looked well, although his face still bore a harrowed expression. A something out of the ordinary in his appearance her eyes soon resolved into the fact that his dark, waving hair, which previously he had always worn rather long and parted in the middle, was so short that it curled closely over his head.

"I've seen the papers," he told her, "and I'm quite flattered to find I'm of enough consequence to have such a fuss made over me just because I left the city for a few days. If I had dreamed there would be this sort of an ado I'd have told you where I was going. But my idea was to keep my whereabouts quiet while I went down into West Virginia, in the mountains, to look into the proposition of developing a marble quarry. I expected when I left to return in three or four days, but it was necessary to go so far on horseback that I couldn't get back that soon and I was so far from the telegraph that I couldn't communicate with you."

"Every one was very anxious, and, down in my heart, I was, too, but I told everybody that it was all right, that you were just away on business and that I expected you back any minute."

"Yes, I saw what a good face you put on it when the reporters insisted on knowing everything you knew, or guessed, or could make up. I'm grateful to you, Miss Marne, for the very sensible stand you took. You showed sense and prudence and did all that you could to stop that absurd fuss. If I should happen to go away again unexpectedly,—" he hesitated, wincing ever so little, but quickly went on: "My deal fell through this time, but I may have to go again, although I hope not, for it's a beastly journey. But if I should, and there should be any disturbance about it, you can say frankly that I've gone to look at some land in the West Virginia mountains, away off the railroad, so that it is impossible to get hold of me until I return to civilization again."

He stopped for a moment, as though turning something over in his mind. "But I don't want to say just where it is," he proceeded cautiously, "because I don't want certain parties to know that I am after this property. And if I don't tell you where it is," and he turned toward her with a pleasant smile and the caressing look in his soft brown eyes that had so much power to stir feminine hearts, "you can truthfully say, if you are asked, that you don't know where I am or how I can be reached."

"How considerate of me he always is," thought Henrietta as she thanked him.

It was not until she had gone through the accumulation of mail with him and had explained to him all that she had done during his absence that he mentioned Hugh Gordon. Then he merely asked, with some hesitation at the name, as though he could with difficulty bring himself to speak it, if no letter had come from him.

"Yes," she replied, unlocking a drawer and taking out a bulky envelope, "this came yesterday, but I guessed that it was from him and so did not open it."

Brand's dark, handsome face turned a trifle paler and his hand trembled as he thrust the letter quickly into his breast pocket.

When the newspapermen came to ask if there were yet any news of him Brand saw them in his own room. He said nothing to Henrietta about the charges made against him by the investigating committee, but in the evening papers and again in those of the next morning she read his defense.

He knew Mr. Flaherty, knew him quite well, he told the reporters, and had had business dealings with him. Mr. Flaherty had advised him about several investments he had thought of making and had helped him in getting some out-of-the-way information concerning them. He had been impressed by the shrewdness of Mr. Flaherty's judgment in these matters, had relied on him a good deal and, altogether, had felt under so much obligation to him that when, after a while, he put a considerable sum of money into Mr. Flaherty's hands for investment, he had insisted upon the politician's taking a more liberal commission than was customary. His idea had been to show his appreciation and relieve himself from any entanglement or obligation. If Mr. Flaherty had chosen to consider it a bribe, he, Felix Brand, could hardly be held responsible for another's idiosyncrasies.

Yes, he had talked with Mr. Flaherty about the municipal art commission and quite possibly had said, in some such conversation, that he would like to be a member of that body because of certain desirable things which it could do, if it would make the effort, for the city's benefit.

He did not know, but he supposed that Mr. Flaherty, agreeing with him about these things and perhaps moved by both public spirit and friendly impulse, had persuaded some of his own friends higher up to suggest his appointment to the commission. He had been, he declared to the newspapermen, surprised and deeply gratified by that appointment and keenly sensible of how great an honor it was, and he had hoped to make his service upon the commission tell for the good of the city.

But he did not wish to hold any position, and especially one so peculiarly delicate in its relations to the public service, under suspicion of any sort of evil practice. And therefore he was willing to resign at once if the investigating committee and the mayor thought they were warranted even in assuming his guilt, although he himself would deeply feel the injustice of such a decision and would be profoundly disappointed should he be unable to make trial of the plans he had been formulating.

The men from the papers were eager to know all that he could, or would, tell them about Hugh Gordon. Had Gordon tried to blackmail him? Was he a relative? What had become of him? Was there anything in Miss Annister's suggestion that Gordon had made a prisoner of him and tried to extract money in that way?

The reporters all noticed that he answered their questions on this subject slowly and with caution. Some of the queries he evaded, some he adroitly ignored, only a few did he meet squarely and fully, and he gave them the very distinct impression that he thought this phase of the matter of no consequence whatever. The sum total of the information they got from him was that he had a very slight acquaintance with "this man Gordon," who, he admitted, was a sort of connection; that he could not exactly say the fellow had tried to blackmail him, although he had made some threats and also had, to express it politely, borrowed money of him; that he had not been held in durance vile during his absence, but had been freely chasing the almighty dollar in a backwoods region of the South; and that he had not the slightest idea whither Gordon had gone, or what had become of him.

And all the time that he talked, and, indeed, through every moment of the day, the one thing of which he was supremely conscious was that bulky envelope that seemed like a weight of lead in his breast pocket. Many times, when he found himself alone, did his hand move quickly toward it. But each time, with a little shudder of repulsion and a furtive glance about the room, his arm fell back and the letter was left untouched. It was not until late in the evening, when he had returned to his apartment and had sat for many minutes alone in his library, his expression telling of a dark and bitter mood, that at last, with sudden resolution, he drew the packet from his breast.

Even then he did not at once open it, but held it in a shaking hand, and stared at it with an angry frown. Once he grasped it in both hands and made as if he would tear it in two. But his fingers stopped with their first movement and his arms dropped.

Springing impatiently to his feet he moved toward the grate as if he would fling the missive upon the coals. But again his will weakened and with a resentful exclamation he walked back to his seat. As he tore the envelope open, he looked up, startled, as if he had heard some unusual sound, gazed about the room, moved the hangings at the window, hurried to the door, which stood ajar, and, after a glance into the next room, closed and locked it. Again he started and stared about him apprehensively. Had he heard, he asked himself, or only imagined, the sound of a scornful, arrogant laugh?

At last, forcing himself to the task, he began to read the letter. It was written in a large, open, round hand that was very legible, notwithstanding the somewhat irregular formation of the letters.

"I went last week to see your mother and sister," it began abruptly, "and you must understand, right now, that you must pay more attention to them. You must have the house repaired and, in general, make them more comfortable—you can see, as well as another, what needs to be done. They would like to have some sign, now and then, that you remember and care about them, and you must give it. I enclose the titles of some books that Penelope would like to read and you must buy them and send them to her at once. I told her you would. And I told them, too, that you are planning to give Penelope a surprise by enclosing one end of the porch with glass so that she can sit there during the winter. You'd better make them a visit over Sunday—next Sunday—and give the order for the work while you are there. Oh, I know that your beauty-loving soul shrinks from having to look at poor, helpless, misshapen Penelope. I understand perfectly well that you much prefer to look at young and pretty women, but my mind is set on this matter. You must do as I—shall we say, suggest?—and that without delay or—there will be consequences. Her poor body is not half so ugly or repulsive as your selfish soul, Felix Brand, and you know very well who is responsible for them both."

As Brand read these last words a quick flush darkened his face, his lips twitched angrily and with a sudden access of wrath he was about to tear the sheet into strips, when his eye caught the next sentence and his countenance paled again as quickly as it had flushed. "And it is my opinion," the letter went on, "that she also is not entirely ignorant on that question."

Brand half rose, crushing the letter in his hand. "Blackguard! I'll read no more of his scurrilous stuff!" he exclaimed with angry emphasis.

52

But the next instant he hesitated, glanced about the room with a sort of dazed uncertainty, then sank into the chair and resumed the letter.

"As you will, doubtless, have learned when you read this, I have done what I told you I would about that municipal art commission affair. You didn't believe I knew enough to carry the thing through successfully. But you know better now. I hope it will convince you that when I make—a suggestion, I mean it and that you'd better follow my advice unless you are willing to take the consequences. That bargaining you did with Flaherty was so idiotic that I lost all patience with you. If you had been willing to wait a while, a year or so, you could have got the position in a perfectly honorable way. But, no! you must have it right now, in order to further your own selfish ends. And so you reach out and snatch it, just as you try to grasp ruthlessly whatever you need or desire for your own purposes. And, as usual, you left the mark of your pitchy fingers. Your soul is so blackly selfish, Felix Brand, that it oozes corruption out of your very finger-ends and contaminates whatever you touch.

"I am much interested in your mother and sister, and I want them to be happy. Unless you do for them more of what it is in your power to do, as I told you before, there will be consequences—I don't know what, just yet, but I can promise you that you will find them unpleasant. I have an eye on several other people also and if it is possible for you to stop any of the mischief you have set going you must do it. It would take too long to speak of all the people you have started in evil ways with your insidious, damnable philosophy, and would probably be useless, too. But there is young Mark Fenlow, on the down grade already, though out of college less than a year. And it was you who put him there.

"Oh, I know how blameless you consider yourself! I know you say it is the right of every one to taste every pleasure within his reach; that it is necessary for one's all-round development to know all sides of life; that it adds not only to one's pleasure, but also to his knowledge of life and so to his personal power to try for himself every possible new experience. You are strong enough to dabble in every filthy pool you encounter, and then to let it alone and go on to another. You live your philosophy and, so far as others can see, although you and I know better, you are none the worse for it. You are a promising young architect, already winning wealth and fame, a charming fellow, a handsome genius, whose friendship is worth having and whose example it is surely all right to follow! But what about those who do follow it and have less will power and perhaps less of that self-control that ambition gives? Are you so hide-bound in your selfishness that you feel no responsibility for them?

"But I know you are. And so I demand that you do something to try to keep Mark Fenlow away from the gaming table and make him understand what will be the outcome of the way he is going now. There's Robert Moreton, too. He begins to look like a dope fiend. I don't know whether he is or not, but he looks it. If he is, it is all because you described to him what a wonderful experience you had when you spent a night in an opium joint and told him he'd better try it, just to see what it was like. I want you to look him up, put him into a sanitarium and, if he needs it, help him financially.

"There are many others, but I can not stop to speak of them all now. Your own conscience ought to tell you of them—if, indeed, you have a conscience, except for me—and move you to try to repair the damage you have done. I insist only that you shall do something, and I'll leave the matter in that shape for the present—until I come again. For I shall come again, Felix Brand, and you can not hinder me. I do not know when, but it will not be long, I promise you.

"I do not know yet just what I shall do. I have been hoping there would be room enough in life for us both. But I begin to doubt that a man so evil as you has the right to live, and big plans are stirring within me. But it will all depend, I think, upon you; upon whether or not you show a desire to overcome your deliberately fostered selfishness and a willingness to recognize your human responsibilities,—upon whether you try to refrain from evil paths yourself and to right the effects of your influence upon others. Yes, I think I can say that the end of all this will depend upon you. And I shall be square with you. I shall do nothing without giving you fair warning and affording you every chance.

"With the money I borrowed of you—willy-nilly, it is true, but still borrowed, for I shall repay it—I intend to go into the real estate business. I have been looking about a little in several cities—New York, Boston, Philadelphia—that was why the reporters could not find me these few days—and have decided where I shall make my beginning and selected the man I shall take into partnership. A week or two when I return, and then it will be plain sailing. I shall repay that compulsory loan with my earliest profits, for I do not choose to be in the least indebted to you.

"As I have what I profoundly feel to be your best interests at heart, and am working for them, I can, with a clear conscience, sign myself,

"Faithfully yours,

"HUGH GORDON."

As Brand read the last lines he sprang to his feet with a sharply indrawn breath and a muttered oath. In his eyes, instead of their habitual soft, affectionate look, was the glitter of a roused animal.

"Impudent devil!" he exclaimed. "Scoundrel! Dictating to me as if he had the right!" He crushed the letter in one fist and, striding across the room, threw it upon the coals with an angry jerk of his arm.

"The fellow used to be amusing," he said to himself, scowling with anger as he watched the sheets blaze up, "but he's getting too insolent to put up with any longer."

His scowl deepened as he watched a word or phrase shine out in the lapping flame, and remembered the context. "Damn you," he cried aloud, whirling about and shaking his fist at the empty room. "I'll take no orders from you! I'll force you back where you belong—and I'll do it in my own way, too!"

CHAPTER VIII

DAYS OF STRESS

The little puff of popular interest in Felix Brand's disappearance and in the charges against him soon disappeared, as some other sensation of a day took its place in the newspaper headlines. People ceased talking about the matter as suddenly as they had begun and Brand congratulated himself that a bank failure, and then a mysterious suicide, and after that an appalling dynamite explosion followed so closely upon his return. He told himself that his own misadventure would speedily be forgotten.

As the weeks went by he became more and more secure in that conclusion. Hugh Gordon did not reappear. And as time passed on and no official action was taken upon the investigating committee's report the architect felt assured that the whole matter had sunk into an oblivion which held no menace for him, and his spirit rose in exultation.

Nor was this the only matter over whose outcome he had reason to be satisfied. All his investments were doing well and his transactions in stocks, during the weeks after his return, brought him money in one good haul after another. And he secured the commission to design a new capitol building for a western state for which there had been lively competition among the most prominent architects of the country.

In her complete loyalty to her employer Henrietta Marne rejoiced to see the harried look leaving his face and his former ease of manner and good spirits return. Knowing, as she did, that his material and professional affairs were fulfilling their earlier promise, she attributed the improvement in his spirits to the apparent sinking out of sight of the man who, she was convinced, had been responsible for all his trouble.

A curious change in Brand's demeanor strengthened her in this conjecture. Something of the spirit of triumph became manifest in his air, his smile was self-confident and in his manner was the assuredness of the man who has won some sort of victory.

His secretary, noting all this with observant but discreet eyes, said to herself that undoubtedly it was all on account of Hugh Gordon. Brand had not mentioned the man's name to her again nor had she learned anything more about his mysterious identity. But she felt sure that he had been trying, from some evil motive, to injure her employer both personally and professionally, and his sudden disappearance, followed by the easing of Brand's anxiety and the betterment of his spirits, convinced her that Gordon had been at the bottom of all the trouble and made her hope that the architect had stopped his machinations and would be annoyed by him no more.

She felt that this Hugh Gordon must be a despicable creature, who tried to do his malevolent work in mean, underhand ways, and when she thought of him it was always with suspicion and enmity.

The winter days sped on and Felix Brand, feeling confident that his footing was once more entirely firm and safe, opened one morning with no misgiving an envelope that bore the stamp of the mayor's office. But even with its first lines his heart, lately so buoyant, turned to lead. It began by saying that doubtless Mr. Brand's duties on the municipal art commission would demand more time and attention than he could bestow upon them in justice to his own exacting private affairs and that therefore whenever he wished to tender his resignation it would receive immediate consideration.

"I shall be sorry," the mayor added, "to lose from that body one who could contribute to the public service so much exact knowledge and artistic feeling; but I have convinced myself that the conclusions of my investigating committee were correct, notwithstanding your denial and plausible explanation. Consequently, I feel that the interests of good government make this step necessary."

Brand was a good deal disturbed by this letter. He had coveted the position much and had been deeply gratified when he received the appointment. For the carrying out of certain plans he had in mind would have brought him prominently into the public eye and secured for him much popular esteem and favor, greatly to the benefit, he believed, of his professional reputation and his income. And now suddenly all these hopes withered and died under the touch of this veiled but peremptory demand for him to get down and out; and he feared that if he did not give quick heed he would have to undergo more publicity of the affair and much humiliation. So he sent at once his letter of resignation.

Soon after this episode Henrietta began to notice in his face again the signs of apprehension and to wonder why he sometimes gave a little nervous start and threw a furtive look about the room.

"Aren't you working too hard, Mr. Brand?" she said to him one day. "You seem to be under such a nervous strain since you began on that capitol building. Don't you think you ought to take a rest before you really give yourself up to it? I'm afraid you won't do yourself justice if you go on with the work while you are in this condition."

He looked at her with his winning, caressing smile of mouth and eyes. "Thank you, Miss Marne. It's kind of you to be so thoughtful about me. A rest would be pleasant, but I couldn't leave, just now, I'm afraid. You know Stewart Macfarlane has asked me to design a country house with big grounds on some property he has bought down toward the south end of Staten Island, and I must go over there soon and study the lay of the land and then begin work on that. And I've got to have the design for that capitol building ready to submit by a certain date. There are three or four unfinished orders on hand and I'm on the track of another public building that I want to land. So I guess it isn't rest I need just now, Miss Marne, so much as a straight course of ten-hour working days. If—if I should have to go South again——"

He straightened up with an impatient jerk, the smile faded from his face and his mouth settled in determined lines. "But I'm not going to take that journey again," he went on impatiently, and then added with decision, "I've settled that."

A few days after this conversation Brand received a letter from the directors of the National Architectural Society suggesting that he resign as president of that body.

"We do not feel," they said, "that our society can afford to continue in that office a man against whom such serious charges of misconduct have been made and who has not asked for an investigation. We do not wish to have the matter exploited publicly any more than is absolutely necessary. To call a general meeting of the society for its discussion would be sure to result in newspaper notice that would doubtless be as disagreeable to you as it would be offensive to us and injurious to our organization. Accordingly, we have decided that the better plan would be for you quietly to resign.

"If you prefer, a general meeting can be called to consider the matter and the society can then decide whether or not to ask for your resignation. The decision rests with you."

Brand immediately replied to the letter, complying with its suggestion in dignified phrases that assured the directors of his loyalty to the best interests of the society, although he was keenly sensitive to the injustice that they were doing him.

"It ought to make them ashamed of themselves," thought Henrietta as she typed the letter. "I never heard of such injustice! They ought to beg his pardon and ask him to keep the office."

No such missive of apology and reparation came, although Henrietta more than half expected it. But Felix Brand cherished no such hope. Instead, premonitions of disaster of which these two episodes would be but the beginning, began to dog his thoughts. His heart was sore with disappointment and mortification, and his breast swelled with bitter resentment against the man whose deliberate action had started this series of events. As he dwelt upon the blasting of his immediate hopes, the smirching of his reputation and the sudden sharp check to the sweeping course of his career, his eyes would burn with hate and anger.

The old look of worry returned to his face, but with it was combined one of grim determination that set in hard lines his usually soft and smiling mouth. Sometimes, Henrietta, coming suddenly into his private office, surprised in his countenance signs of fear. But what she oftenest saw there was the look of dogged resolution. She began to be conscious, too, of some sort of struggle going on within him.

She could see it in these unaccustomed expressions of his countenance, hear it in the petulant voice in which he sometimes addressed her, so different from his usual suave tones, and feel it in the nervous strain under which he was evidently laboring.

As the days went by the very atmosphere in which they worked seemed to her to grow tense with it, and on days when it was necessary for her to be much in his room she would go home in the evening with her own nerves quivering from its influence.

On a day in early March, a bracing day of brilliant sky, clear air and sharp west wind, Brand said to Henrietta when he left the office for luncheon that probably he would not return in the afternoon. "I think," he said, "that I shall go across to Staten Island and motor down to Macfarlane's property and get a general idea of the site and the surroundings."

"A splendid idea," she assented with enthusiasm. "It's such a fine day, the ride will do you good."

"Do you think," he said with a smile, "that your sister would bear me company?"

"I'm sure she would be delighted," Henrietta smiled back, and not until an hour later did she remember, with a little qualm of doubtfulness, Mildred Annister's evident jealousy of their previous motor ride.

"Dear Mildred!" she thought. "She is so completely wrapped up in her love. I wish Dr. Annister would consent for them to be married soon. It would make Mildred so happy and I'm sure it would be a good thing for Mr. Brand."

When Henrietta reached home she found her sister only just returned, and in high spirits. At dinner, her eyes sparkling and her cheeks flushed with delicate pink, her droll little stories, and her merry laughter kept them all in a gay humor.

"We've had such a good time this evening," said Mrs. Marne when, at her early bedtime, she bade Henrietta goodnight. "Wasn't Bella charming! And so pretty she looked with her bright eyes and that dainty color in her cheeks! It made me wish Warren was here to see her. I suppose I'm dreadfully old-fashioned, Harry, but it always seems to me that if a woman is looking especially beautiful or charming it's somehow just wasted if the man who loves her isn't there to see it. Wasn't it kind of Mr. Brand to take Bella out this afternoon! And she did enjoy it so much! I can't be grateful enough that you were so fortunate as to get a position under such a thorough gentleman!"

Billikins was Henrietta's dog and her particular care. When she went to the kitchen to feed him after dinner she found him licking many gaping wounds in the body and clothing of his cherished plaything, the rag-doll. Delia had an excited story to tell her of his disreputable conduct during the afternoon.

"It was very queer and strange, Miss Harry, the way he acted when Mr. Brand was here. An' him always such a mild and innocent little dog! Of course he had to run into the hall when the bell rang, like he always does, to see what's happening, with babykins in his mouth, and as I went upstairs to call Miss Bella, he trotted into the parlor where I'd shown the gentleman. An' when I come down you just ought to've heard the wild an' awful noises he was making! He'd dropped his doll and was whining an' howling an' growling, and he'd run toward Mr. Brand an' bark an' growl, and then he'd run back and stand over babykins as if he was afraid something would happen to her, an' growl an' whine an' bark! I called him and he wouldn't pay no attention to me and I had to go in and pick him up and carry him out, him an' babykins together, and bring them out here. And he tried to go back and I shut the door and then he crouched down beside it and worried babykins an' tore holes in her an' whined an' growled an' trembled as if he was most scared to death. Now, wasn't it queer and strange, Miss Harry?"

Billikins had stopped eating and was looking up into their faces as if he understood what they were talking about. Henrietta bent over him and he crept whining to her feet and looked up at her with dumb appeal in his eyes, as though begging to be saved from some mysterious, menacing, unseen thing. She took him up in her arms and felt his little body trembling with fear and excitement. Vivid recollection came to her of how her own nerves had quivered and jangled in the office that day, as long as her employer was there, until it had taken all her strength to keep them under control.

"Poor little doggie," she said, stroking and cuddling him. "Come along and we'll take babykins upstairs and sew her all up as good as new and forget all about it."

"So that was the man you work for, Miss Harry!" Delia exclaimed as Henrietta turned to leave the room. "I was dusting in the parlor when he come an' I watched him as he come up the walk, and he's got a firm and manly tread. He's fine-legged and handsome, Miss Harry, but if I was you I'd be afraid of a man that a dog's afraid of, Miss Harry."

"We had such a jolly time," said Isabella to her sister as Henrietta came to her room for a confidential chat during bedtime toilette rites. "Felix Brand is just the loveliest ever. But you know I always did think that, even before I met him. Mother was having her afternoon nap when he came and I was doubtful about going. But he said, nonsense, she'd sleep till I'd get back.

"At first I couldn't help feeling a little uneasy about her and perhaps I was a tiny bit glum and not as entertaining as he thought I'd be. And he seemed sort of glum and grim, too, and, altogether, Harry, on the first lap the ride didn't promise to be entirely successful.

"But after a while he was afraid I was cold and said we must find something to warm us up. So we stopped at the Wayside Tavern—you remember it, don't you? You know we went there on the trolley last summer and took a long walk into the woods and had some lemonade on the porch while we waited for the car on our way back. Well, we went in there and this time it was champagne——"

"Bella! You didn't, did you?"

"Of course I did! Why not?"

"It doesn't seem to me quite a—a nice thing for a girl to do, Bella."

"Oh, nonsense, Harry! What's the matter with it? Anyway, there wasn't anything the matter with the champagne; nor with the rest of our ride either. We went to the Macfarlane place and circled round it and he told me some of the things he is going to do there, and then we did some speeding that was—oh, Harry, we fairly flew! It was just grand! And I guess my tongue went, too, for he talked and laughed and was as gay as could be. I forgot all about poor mother until we sighted home again. But I never had such a good time in all my life."

CHAPTER IX

BATTLING WITH THE INVISIBLE

It seemed to his secretary the next day that Felix Brand was in a calmer mood. She had become accustomed to read with ease his tell-tale countenance, through which shone so plainly his states of mind and feeling, and the first anxious glance she cast upon him with her morning greeting relieved her forebodings of another trying day.

The signs of inward struggle were no longer manifest, though the same dogged resolution still sharpened the lines of his face, and it was evident that he was more able to concentrate himself upon his work than he had been for many days. Whatever the trouble was that had barked and snapped so incessantly about him that his combat with it had distracted his attention and engrossed his energies, for the present at least, it seemed to be cast aside. In the late afternoon Henrietta heard him make an engagement over the telephone with Mildred Annister.

Before he left the office, as he was signing the letters she had typed, he stopped over one, after writing his name, and considered it for a moment. It was concerned with an effort he was making to get control of the marble quarry in which he was interested.

"No," he said, "I'll leave this matter until tomorrow. Please call my attention to it in the morning, if I should happen not to think of it. And there are some books, here is a list of them, which I should like to have here, ready to consult, the first thing tomorrow. You may send the boy for them now and leave them on my desk. These two he may buy, but the others have him get from the library. If any of these shouldn't be in have him buy those also, for I particularly want to have them ready for use as soon as I get here. And I shall probably," he added, looking at her with his pleasant smile as he picked up his hat and gloves, "work you very hard tomorrow looking up references and finding things for me that I remember to have seen somewhere inside the covers of those books."

Henrietta went home much pleased by the favorable turn affairs had taken. The better prospect for her own personal comfort had its share in her gratification. But it was small beside her relief that her employer seemed to have won through his besetting harassments and, his pleasant, winning self again, was once more earnestly devoting himself to his affairs. For these had suffered during the last few weeks, while his absorption in his hidden troubles not only had kept him from devoting proper attention to them, but even had seemed to dull his capacities. He himself had felt that his artistic perceptions, usually so true and keen, were blunted and blurred. Upon the design for one of his commissions, a country house in the Berkshires, he had made beginning after beginning, only to throw each one aside in disgust and discouragement. Nor had the various other orders in hand advanced much better. He had not even begun the design for the capitol building, although he was under contract to have it finished in three months.

Henrietta knew that he was beginning to feel worried about the unsatisfactory trend of his work and she had been watching the course of affairs with secret anxiety. She knew, too, that recently he had been disappointed and annoyed by several business matters. He prided himself upon his acute business sense, but lately he had blundered more than once in his orders to his stock brokers and had lost some money.

But, puzzled though she was by these developments in Felix Brand's character and temperament and apprehensive of their results, if she could have witnessed the scene that was taking place in his apartment ten or twelve hours after he bade her that smiling farewell for the day, far greater would have been her alarm and bewilderment.

It was well toward morning, but every light in every room was shining at its brightest. From one room to another, from end to end of the suite and back again, its master was walking rapidly, constantly, as if he feared to stop for an instant or even to check his pace. The light, muffled sound of his hurried tread barely disturbed the silence that hung, close and heavy, over the rooms; that brooding silence of the late hours of the night which seems to have hushed all the sounds that ever were, but out of which almost any sound might be born.

As he rushed through drawing room, chambers, dining room, library, like another Wandering Jew urged pitilessly, incessantly, back and forth in a contracted round, not another living eye did his own encounter in the brilliantly lighted rooms. He was entirely alone. But every now and then his voice rang sharply through the stillness in angry, resentful, resolute tones.

"You shall not! You shall not!" he shouted, shaking his fist at the empty air and squaring his shoulders as though he expected some ghostly enemy to materialize from behind a door or out of the folds of a portiere.

He threw off his coat and waistcoat and, wiping the sweat from his face, hurried on again in his ceaseless round.

In the dining room he halted at the sideboard and filled a glass with brandy and soda. It was his custom to drink sparingly at all times and when alone he rarely touched liquor of any sort. So now, when he saw how much of the brandy bottle was empty, he gave a low whistle of amazement.

"What!" he exclaimed. "Have I drank all that tonight? And I wouldn't know that I'd taken a drop!"

He swallowed the mixture eagerly, as if it were some elixir from which he expected to gain new strength, and turned back upon his tramp. As he passed through his bedroom his gaze longingly sought the bed and his steps wavered toward it. His eyelids yearned for sleep and his strength was ebbing. With a stiffening of his muscles and a clenching of his fists he held himself steadily on his course.

"No, you don't," he muttered. "I won't give in! Do you hear me? I will not give in!"

He marched on, his head thrust forward, his mouth set hard in dogged determination and his hands clenched in his pockets. As he passed through the library he suddenly wavered and a spasm of apprehension crossed his face. He paused uncertainly for a moment, then strode to the entrance door of the apartment, made sure that it was locked, and brought the key back with him. A gleam of triumph mingled with the fear and anxiety in his face and eyes as he turned the combination lock of a little safe set in the wall behind a screen. The door swung open and with a smile of exultation he put the key inside and was about to close the door again when he stopped short, and, as if with the flashing of some new thought, his whole face and figure sagged.

"What's the use?" he muttered disappointedly. "He probably knows this combination, damn him, as well as I do!"

Anger rose in a quick flood and with a wrathful oath he flung the key on the floor. His face was grimmer and more resolute than before as he whirled about and rushed from the room. Already pale and drawn, it went a shade whiter with the effort of will that kept him on his feet and still moving. At the door of the drawing room his hands flew upward to the height of his shoulders and doubled into fists. His eyes were fixed in a blank stare and his face was working in a mortal agony.

"Ah-h-h!" he gasped.

And then: "There!" he cried in a triumphant tone, as with one foot he sent spinning across the room the chair beside which he had halted. His breast was heaving and his breath coming hard as he looked this way and that with wild eyes. Throwing open a window he put out his head and caught the cold air upon his streaming face. The sky was brightening with the promise of dawn.

"Good God!" he groaned as he turned back into the room. "Why did I try to stick this out alone? Why didn't I do something, go somewhere, have some of the fellows come here to an all-night game? Oh, I was afraid—that's the truth, I was afraid—and you knew it, damn you, you knew it!" he ended in angry tones.

In the library he looked wistfully toward his favorite easy chair, for his knees trembled with weariness. "No, no, I must not stop. If I sat down I'd go to sleep, and then——"

He wheeled about and started back. But he held his head higher and walked with a more confident air. "I'm winning," he exclaimed, and there was glad surety in his voice. "It was a close call, but I'm winning! Get back to where you belong, you dog! Go back to where you came from, damn you, and stay there! I've won, I tell you!" And he stamped his foot and cried again, "I've won!"

But confident though he was of having won this victory, whatever it might be, over the invisible enemy whom he seemed both to hate and to fear, he did not yet dare to cease from his tramp. Back and forth he still went; and presently, pausing beside the open window, he saw that the sky was flushed with sunrise and heard the roar and rattle of another day rising from the streets.

"A bath soon, and breakfast," he thought, "and then out for the day, and I'll be fairly safe once more. And if things get hard, I'll motor over to Staten Island and take Miss Marne's sister out again. That experiment helped a lot yesterday."

He went through the rooms, putting up shades and pushing back curtains and switching off electric lights. His face was white and haggard and in his eyes still lingered the look of wild anxiety which had filled them for so many hours. With hands that trembled he poured another glass of brandy and soda. As he passed the door of his chamber his step lagged, he turned and looked in.

"No! No!" he cried harshly, and tried to walk on. But his feet were like lead and held him there. Once more his body stiffened for battle, his teeth ground together and his lips shut in a straight, hard line.

He staggered a little way toward the bed, trying to hold himself back, as if he were wrestling, with all his remnant of strength and will, against some immaterial, compelling force. Striking out with one fist, as at some foe beside him, he shouted thickly, "Go! Go back, I say!" And with a supreme effort he wheeled about and with uncertain, heavy steps moved back toward the door.

"I will not! I will not!" he muttered, his voice unsteady and anguished. From his face had faded the determined look and his eyes, glassy and staring, were turned upward in terrified appeal.

Even as he spoke his feet once more refused to move. They seemed rooted to the floor, but his body, though he tried his best still to face toward the entrance, turned again toward the bed. He caught at the door and braced himself against it for a moment. Then his grasp weakened and his arms fell down.

The clutching will that was battling with his moved him one step, and then another, toward the end that he feared, though he strove so fiercely against it that the sinews of his neck seemed about to burst through their restraining skin. Stiffening his body, catching at chairs and tables and putting all his strength into the effort to hold his feet firm upon the floor, he fought with the intangible force that gripped him.

"I will not! I will not!" he gasped; and with a mighty effort tore himself from his bonds and rushed toward the door. But again viewless hands seized him and turned him suddenly about. His haggard face flushed to a dull red and beaded with sweat as he fought with the unseen power that impelled him, step by step, across the room.

With breath coming in gasps, he struggled on desperately, sometimes gaining a little space and again losing more; and seeing himself, despite his utmost efforts, forced nearer and nearer to the goal that he knew meant his vanquishment. Inch by inch he fought the way with his invisible enemy to the very bedside. Even there, with his last ounce of strength, he made a final, futile effort to break away from his intangible captor. Then he flung up his arms and covered his face and with a long "oh-h-h," that was half a rageful, hysterical cry and half a moan of despair, he sank face downward upon the bed.

He had lost the battle in what he had thought to be the very hour of victory.

He Sank Face Downward Upon the Bed

CHAPTER X

HUGH GORDON WINS HENRIETTA'S CONFIDENCE

Henrietta reached the office early that morning, lest her employer, in his eagerness to push his work, now that he could devote himself to it with undivided energies, should get there first. She looked forward to the day with pleasant anticipations, for she had assisted him in this way before and she liked it the best of all her duties. The books were ready upon his desk, but he had not yet arrived. She waited for him all the forenoon, employing herself as best she could, and still he did not come.

In the afternoon she tried to get his apartment on the telephone, but there was no answer. Surely, he would not have left the city, after such preparations for a busy day, without sending her some message. She called up Dr. Annister and asked if he had seen Mr. Brand that day, or knew whether or not he had unexpectedly gone out of the city. No, the doctor replied, he had not seen Mr. Brand since the evening before, when he and Mildred and Mrs. Annister had gone to the theatre together. As Mildred had been looking quite happy all day he did not think Felix could have said anything about going out of town. And he had promised to dine with them tomorrow night. Doubtless if he had gone anywhere it was only for the day and Dr. Annister was cheerfully confident Henrietta might expect to see him again on the morrow.

She lingered at the office an hour later than usual, hoping for some word from the architect. But none came. The next morning she hurried back, eagerly anticipating a letter or a telegram, but found neither. All day she waited, her nerves on edge with expectation and anxiety, but Brand did not come nor did he send her any message.

"This is worse than it was before," thought Henrietta, "for then he told me beforehand that he might have to go. And he said so positively, only a little while ago, that he did not intend to take that trip south again. Perhaps he found he had to go after all. Anyway, I guess it's what I'd better tell people."

Remembering his dinner engagement at Dr. Annister's, she made that explanation over the telephone. Both to Dr. Annister and afterward to Mildred she said that she did not know positively that he had gone to West Virginia, but that he had told her, when he returned from his former absence, that that was where he had been and that he might have to go again, although he had not told her the exact place because, for business reasons, he did not want it to be known.

Yes, Mildred assented, he had said the same thing to her and she understood just how it was. But all the same, it was cruel of Felix, and not at all like him, for he was always so sweetly considerate, to go off in this sudden, secret way and leave them all in such suspense.

"When we're married," and a happy little laugh came rippling over the telephone to Henrietta's ear, "it shan't be like this, for then he'll have to take me with him on all such jaunts and I'll see to it that you know where we are."

As the days went by, Henrietta, pondering with ever increasing anxiety the mystery of this second disappearance, began to doubt the explanation she gave to others. This time there came up no reason for public interest and so even the knowledge that he was away was confined to a few of his friends and to those who wished to see him upon business. With all inquirers his secretary treated his absence as an ordinary matter, saying merely that she thought he was somewhere in the mountains of West Virginia, she did not know exactly where, nor could she say positively when he would be back.

Nevertheless, looking back over what he said to her on his return after his previous long absence, Henrietta recognized in it a touch of insincerity. At the time she had accepted it as a matter of course, but now, scrutinizing her memory of his words and his manner, in the light of all that had happened since, she finally said to herself, "I don't believe he was telling me the truth."

But if that southern business trip was a deliberate fabrication, what, then, could be the reason for a prolonged absence, so injurious to all his interests, whose real nature and purpose he had been at such pains to conceal? She had heard of men who sometimes slipped out of sight that they might plunge unhampered into debauchery, and she began to wonder if such were the case with him, or if, perhaps, he had fallen a victim to some secret vice. But against either of these suppositions both her feminine instincts and her personal liking for her employer rebelled.

"I don't see how that could be," she thought, "for he is always so nice and refined. There is no suggestion about him of anything gross or so—unclean. No, it can't be anything of that sort. And yet, he seemed so nervous, and just as if he were fighting against something with all his might—and I suppose it would be like that if he were fighting the desire to drink or take some kind of dope. But I can't believe it. I wonder if that Hugh Gordon could have anything to do with it. Well, whatever the explanation, it's evident he doesn't want people to know about his being away, and he doesn't like it to be talked about, so the thing for me to do is to keep as still as a mouse and not to let anybody else do any more talking than I can help."

Even at home, in her loyalty to her sense of duty, Henrietta said no more than to make a mere mention of her employer's absence and to reply, when her mother or sister made occasional inquiry, that he had not yet returned.

Brand had been away almost a week when the office boy brought her a card one morning and said the gentleman was particularly anxious to see her. As she looked at it and read "Hugh Gordon" her heart began to beat faster and her face flushed a sudden red.

Had he come, she wondered, to bring her news of Brand's whereabouts, or, perhaps, tidings of some serious misfortune? The apprehensive thought flashed through her mind that perhaps he would try, under threat of evil to herself or her employer, to force from her some personal or business information that he could afterward use as a lever against the architect, and she told herself that she must be very careful what she said to him.

She felt assured that he was there for no good purpose, and during the moment that she waited for the boy to bring him into her room her mind formed a swift picture of an elderly fellow, slouching and shabby, red-nosed and unshaven, bearing all the marks of a parasitic and dissipated life.

When she saw instead a well-groomed young man, wearing an English looking gray suit, advancing toward her with a quick, firm step and a self-confident air, the reversal of her preconceived ideas was so complete that for an instant she thought it must be some one else. The suggestion of a smile crossed his serious face as he met her disconcerted look and, halting beside her desk, he repeated his name.

"I have come to see you, Miss Marne, to relieve your mind of any apprehension you may feel concerning Mr. Felix Brand."

"Oh," she exclaimed, the reassurance his words gave her evident at once in her voice. "Then you have seen him? You know that he is quite well?"

His keen, dark eyes swept the room with an alert glance. On her desk glowed a vase of sunshine-colored daffodils. She remembered afterward that, while his one swift glance had seemed to take in everything in the room, it had passed over the flowers as coolly as it had over the chairs and the typewriter, and she compared it with the way Felix Brand's eyes would have lingered and feasted upon them.

"I have not seen him for several days," he replied, his gaze again straight into her eyes. He spoke rapidly, in a direct, almost blunt manner. "But I can assure you that you need to feel no anxiety about him. He is quite safe and will be back here as soon as circumstances permit."

Henrietta hesitated for an instant, in quick debate with herself as to the most prudent course to pursue. Should she try to find out all that this man knew, or, refusing to admit how much she was in the dark herself, thank him for his kindness in such a way as to make him believe she did not need his information? She was aware already she was not so suspicious of him as she had been a few moments before. The friendly sincerity of his look and the blunt frankness of his manner compelled her into a less wary, less hostile feeling. Reminding herself again that she must be on her guard she motioned him to a chair beside her desk.

"You must know, Mr. Gordon," she said, looking at him with a gaze as direct as his own, "that your attitude toward Mr. Brand some weeks ago was not such as to make me feel, now, much confidence in your good intentions. Frankly, I find it difficult to believe that you have come here with his good in view."

Gordon's serious countenance relaxed a little and Henrietta felt herself impelled to a responsive smile, which she quickly checked.

"No," he agreed, "I can't expect you, not knowing all the circumstances, to understand that what I did then was intended for Felix Brand's good. I believed, or at least I hoped, that it would have a salutary effect upon him and induce him to turn back from a course of conduct that I foresaw would be disastrous."

He straightened up and his dark eyes, that would have been somber but for their keenness, ran quickly down over her face and figure and then rested again with a softened expression upon hers.

"I would like you to believe that, whatever was the result of what I did, I had no evil or selfish motive in doing it. Can you feel that much confidence in me, Miss Marne?"

She bent her eyes upon the desk for the moment of silence that followed his question and made effort to voice her reply in a cool, disinterested tone.

"I can understand that you might have been moved by a sense of duty toward the public welfare—if you believed in your own assertions. I gather from what you said just now that you wish to be considered Mr. Brand's friend; but that sort of thing does not agree with my idea of the loyalty there should be between friends."

His black brows drew together in a slight frown as he looked intently at her averted face. "Well," he said, more slowly than he had previously spoken, "I shall not try to justify myself. I shall only repeat that my motive was neither selfish nor malicious. I had not thought particularly, in fact, I had not thought at all then, about the public side of it. I did it solely in the hope that it would have a good effect upon Felix." He paused again for a moment and as she noted his familiar use of her employer's name she thought that, after all, the relations between them must be intimate.

"But I hope," he went on, his manner again brusque, "that you will free your mind from all suspicion as to my reasons for coming here today."

She flushed and turned a little more away, and he smiled behind his hand as he stroked his short, thick, black mustache.

"I know already more about Felix Brand and his affairs than pleases me and I am just now much more interested in my own."

She faced him with a sudden movement and asked sharply: "Do you know where he is?"

Her eyes caught an inscrutable change in his. Something almost like awe came into them and into his countenance as his gaze turned to the window and sought the blue and distant sky.

"No," he said, his voice sounding a solemn note, and repeated: "No, I do not. I do not know where he is now."

His eyes returned to her face and as he met her startled expression he exclaimed in a kindly way, leaning forward as if to reassure her: "There! I've frightened you! Please don't be alarmed. I assure you, there's nothing to be anxious about. Although I don't know positively where Felix is, just now, I do know he has suffered no harm, no real harm, and I believe, I am quite sure, he will be back here again as well as ever, before very long. I came here to tell you this."

She studied his face for a moment and somehow, against her will, the conviction came upon her that this man was moved, as he declared, by good motives.

"It was kind of you," she replied at last with a gracious smile, "and I thank you very much. I was quite anxious, but I believe what you have told me and I am greatly relieved."

He looked pleased and exclaimed impulsively: "And I thank you for your confidence in me!"

As he rose to go, his glance once more traveled quickly down over her face and figure and returned to her eyes with a look in his own that her woman's instinct knew to mean appreciation, interest, liking.

"By the way," he said, turning impulsively toward her and speaking in a quick, brusque way, "there is another matter I must not forget. It was part of my reason for coming here. There was a letter—you remember—that Felix had you write the last day he was here and then asked you not to send just then. You haven't mailed it yet, have you?"

She stared at him in astonishment and said "No," before she could take counsel of her caution.

"I didn't suppose you had. However, I happen to know, he told me, that he would like you to send it at once, just as it stands now."

Henrietta was so astounded by this revelation of the intimacy that must exist between the two men that for a moment she could not reply. For the letter was concerned with an effort Brand was making to get control of the marble quarry company in which he had invested some months before, and she knew that he was keeping the matter very secret and considered it of great importance. It had worried her more than anything else in his arrested affairs, for she hesitated to mail it without farther instructions from him and yet had feared that if she did not his plans might fall through.

Gordon went on without appearing to notice her surprise, although she felt sure that he saw it and was amused by it. "As you know, he wanted to wait a day or two for certain developments at the other end."

Henrietta nodded. "Yes, and I have not been able to find out just what happened."

"It's all right—just as Felix hoped it would be," he assured her and went on to tell her briefly what had occurred.

After his departure Henrietta found herself comparing her visitor with her employer. All her previous thought of Gordon had been in connection with Brand as the cause of his troubles, as his enemy and even his persecutor. So now, when Gordon appeared in person, it was against a contrasting background of the appearance and character of the man to whom she felt so grateful for the opportunity of livelihood amid congenial surroundings.

Gordon was much in her mind during the rest of the day; and as she traveled homeward in the afternoon, in the subway, across the ferry in the glowing sunset light, and in the clattering trolley car, her thought was busy with speculation about him, with comparison of him with Felix Brand, with recollections of what he had said and how he had looked, with conjecture as to the meaning of his expression when she asked him if he knew where Brand was.

At dinner she spoke of her caller to her mother and sister. At once they were interested and were eager to know what he was like and what Henrietta thought of him. As she answered their questions she felt her cheeks flushing when she saw their surprise that she should praise or seem to admire the man who was Felix Brand's enemy.

"I know you are surprised," she said, trying to overcome a sudden access of self-consciousness, "that he isn't at all the sort of man we thought him, or at least that I was sure he must be. But it was certainly considerate of him to come, and there was nothing at all in anything he said or did that suggested a different motive. I never was more surprised in my life than I was by his appearance. You know Mr. Brand told the reporters that he is a relative and I had supposed he must be some dissipated, disreputable sort of creature. And then in came this good-looking young man—for he is good-looking, though not so handsome as Mr. Brand—his face hasn't that look of refinement and affability. He was well-dressed and looked like a prosperous young business man, and he has such a straightforward, independent air."

"Does he look like Mr. Brand?" queried Isabella, so interested that she was forgetting her dinner.

"A little—yes. In some ways a good deal, and then again he seems so different. He is dark and his features have a family resemblance. But otherwise the two men are not alike. You know that dear expression Mr. Brand's eyes always have, so winning and affectionate, and as if he thought the world of you. Well, Mr. Gordon's eyes are large and brown, too, but they are keen and they look right through you and he flashes one glance around the room and you feel that he knows everything in it. He isn't so polished in his manners——"

"Mr. Brand has the loveliest manners of any man I ever met," Isabella interrupted. "His mission in life ought to be to travel round and show them off as a pattern for all other young men. I wish Warren could have the advantage of a few lessons."

"Bella!" exclaimed her mother reprovingly. "You ought not to speak that way of the man who is almost your husband. And Warren is such a good man, too!"

"So is Mr. Brand," Isabella replied saucily, "awfully good, just too good to be true. Tell us more about Mr. Gordon, Harry."

"Why, as I was saying, his manner isn't so polished as Mr. Brand's. In fact, he is so direct and positive that he seems a little curt, though I'm sure he doesn't mean to be. He makes you feel that he's very sincere, too. Mr. Brand seems to draw people to him without making any effort, but Mr. Gordon is more compelling and something about him makes you take an interest in him and believe in him."

"He impressed you a good deal, didn't he, Harry?" said Isabella, looking at her sister thoughtfully.

Henrietta felt her cheeks warming again and was annoyed at herself that she should blush in this way when, as she scolded herself, "there was no reason for it."

"I don't know that he did, particularly," she said defensively. "His coming was rather curious and you and mother seemed interested and wanted to know all about him."

CHAPTER XI

PENELOPE HAS A VISITOR

Penelope Brand lay back in her wheel-chair in the glass-enclosed porch and gave herself up to luxurious enjoyment of its sun-filled warmth. The table beside her with its books and its sewing, but just now finished and neatly folded, gave evidence that she had spent a busy morning. Outside there was bright sunshine, too, but there was also a raw March wind that filled the air with dust and stimulated the tear-ducts of the eyes that faced it. The little glass porch had brought a very great pleasure into her life, giving her, during the shut-in winter season, always hard for her to endure, wider views of earth and sky, a flood of the sunshine in which she loved to bask and, on days when it was possible to keep the entrance open, much more fresh air.

She sat there alone, loving the sunny warmth and thinking of the brother who had made her pleasure possible. Her secret mental attitude toward him was marked by a certain aloofness and a quietly judicial estimate which she did her best to conceal from her mother. It had cost her not a little effort, too, to keep this attitude from developing into stern censorious judgment. Just now it added to her pleasure that her feeling toward him, at least for the time being, could be mainly that of gratitude, though gratitude tempered by curiosity.

"Perhaps he'd have done it long ago if I had asked him," she told herself. "And I've longed for something of the sort so much. I do wonder what made him finally think of it himself. It wasn't like him. He might have thought of it and wanted to do it ten or twelve years ago, before he had plenty of money. But it's not like him now."

The click of the gate attracted her attention and she saw a man coming up the walk. "Why, that can't be Felix," she thought in doubting surprise. Then, as she looked at him more attentively, "Oh, no! It's that Mr. Gordon who was here last winter. Felix didn't seem to like very well his calling on us. And mother isn't at home. Well,

I'll have to see him. And perhaps it's just as well, for I don't care particularly whether Felix likes it or not."

He held her thin, talon-like hand affectionately as he asked how she was and if she enjoyed her glass cage.

"Enjoy it! Oh, Mr. Gordon! You can't imagine how I delight in it! I sit here most of the time every day in all kinds of weather. It has given me the greatest pleasure, and I think I am better and stronger, too, because of it. I was just thinking how grateful I am to Felix."

His face and eyes, which had been glowing with responsive pleasure, darkened at her last sentence.

"I don't like that word 'grateful' in connection with such a matter," he exclaimed quickly. "It was a little thing for Felix to do, only one out of all the many things that he could do for you if he would, and one that he ought to have done long ago. And it doesn't seem to me, Penelope, that *you* would have any reason to be 'grateful' to Felix Brand, no matter how much he might do for you."

The significant tone in which he spoke the last words brought surprise into her face. She turned toward him with astonished inquiry in her dark eyes, but, as she met his assured gaze, that expression quickly changed into one of understanding. It was evident that she knew what he meant. She looked at him steadily for a moment, a moment of inner effort in which she brought her own impulse of responsive feeling under firmer control, before she replied:

"Wouldn't that be a barbarian sort of philosophy to live by?"

"Perhaps it would," he admitted, paused an instant, and then went on with some heat:

"But when I think of all that you have suffered because of him, and how little he has tried to make amends, I am so indignant that merely refraining to be 'grateful' for such a crumb as this seems nothing to what he deserves."

A faint color crept into her thin, pale cheeks as again she stared at him wide-eyed.

"I know all about it," he continued, nodding at her gravely. "I know that you would have been as straight and strong as any girl, and a noble, capable, active woman, if he hadn't pushed you off the limb of that apple-tree in your back yard twenty years ago, because he was determined to have your place."

"Did he tell you about it?" she demanded, her voice trembling with excitement. "But he must have, because nobody else, not even father or mother, ever knew. They thought I fell."

"Yes, I know that was the version he gave of the affair, and everybody accepted it. And you kept the truth to yourself."

"What good would it have done to blame him after it was all over? And he didn't intend to do it."

"Yes, he did! He meant to push you off and get your place and show you that he was boss."

"Perhaps, but he had no intention of hurting me—he didn't think that it would."

"Oh, I know he had no murderous purpose. He just gave up to a selfish, brutal impulse, and afterwards he was too cowardly and too selfish to confess the truth."

She turned upon him a steady, wondering gaze and he shrank back a little and went on more humbly:

"I suppose I ought not to speak in that way to you about your brother, and I hope you will pardon me. But when I compare your life with his it makes me too indignant to keep a bridle on my tongue. And, besides, Penelope," and he leaned toward her with his manner again forceful with the strength of his convictions, "you know as well as I do how truthful is every word I have said."

"And even if I do," she rejoined with dignity, "it is possible that I would not choose to admit all that my secret heart might think."

She stopped with a little start and a drawing together of her brows, and then, with alarm dawning in her eyes, she leaned forward eagerly and put a pleading hand upon his arm:

"You won't say anything about this to mother, will you?"

Gordon hesitated, but his eyes, flashing with the intensity of his feeling, softened as they fell upon her anxious face.

"It's hardly fair," he said doggedly, "it certainly isn't just, for her to glorify Felix as she does when he is—what he is. In justice to you she ought to know this."

"That's of no consequence at all beside the pain it would give her to know the truth. You don't know mother—nobody does but me—and you can't appreciate in the least what Felix, or, rather, her ideal of Felix, means to her. Mother is, and always has been, a romantic sort of woman, as you might guess"—and she smiled faintly at him—"by the names she gave her children. Her own life has been hard and monotonous, with little pleasure, little beauty—and she has such a beauty-loving nature—little opportunity. And she is so shy, too, she has so little self-confidence. So, don't you see, all the romance and imagination that have been starved in her have been born over again for her in Felix. Felix is handsome, magnetic—he attracts people and makes everybody his friends, as she would have liked to do—he is a genius, he creates beautiful things, he lives in lovely surroundings, he is winning fame and wealth—life for him is a Grand Adventure, more beautiful and wonderful than anything she ever dared to dream. She knows Felix is selfish, but she can always see so many reasons why it is impossible for him to do any particular generous thing. Oh, Mr. Gordon, it would grieve her so to know how that accident really happened and how he concealed the truth and— and——"

"Ah, you don't like to say it," he broke in as she hesitated and ceased speaking. "But I know what you mean—how he profited by it. For the money that would have been divided upon the education of both of you if you had been well and strong was all spent upon him. And he took it and kept silent."

Again she stared at him in surprise. "How frankly Felix must have talked with you!" she exclaimed. "He never would have confessed all this if he hadn't felt remorseful and repentant!"

"But he isn't!" Gordon blurted out with an irritated start. "He's come to think it a part of his good fortune. If he had been, or, even, if he were now — well, things might have turned out differently — that's all I can say."

"But we're getting away from mother. Don't you see, Mr. Gordon, that it would be cruel? And what good would it do? Felix is what he is, and he'll stay so to the end of the chapter. You can't change him and you would only spoil mother's happiness in him. Promise me, Mr. Gordon, that you won't tell her anything about it, that you won't say anything to her about Felix that would make her unhappy!"

Gordon rose abruptly and walked across the little enclosure and back again, his black brows drawn together, before he replied.

"It is hard to refuse you anything, Penelope," he said finally, standing in front of her chair. "You have had so little, and you deserve so much. I know you are right about this, and I shrink from hurting her as much as you do. But when I think of Felix and the course he has deliberately followed, it angers me so that I forget everything except the retribution he so richly deserves. But you are right and I give you your promise."

He smiled upon her and gently patted the hand that lay, thin and feeble-looking, on the arm of her chair. But the smile quickly faded from his face as he met the mingled wonder and displeasure of her look.

"I thank you for your promise," she said, "but I am surprised to hear you speak so bitterly of my brother, when you seem to be so friendly with him and he has given you such intimate confidence."

Again Gordon walked up and down in the narrow space, his countenance somber with the intentness of his thought.

"The relations between us are peculiar," he said at last, speaking more slowly and deliberately than was usual with him. "I wonder if

I could tell you what they are. I wonder if you would believe me, or think me sane, if I should tell you. Sometime I shall tell you, Penelope, for you are a broad-minded, strong-souled woman and you will be able to see that what I am doing has been for the best good of everybody concerned. But I think not now. No, not yet, not till after I have worked out my plan. But I want you to know, Penelope, and I shall never be content until you do understand. For I honor and admire you more than anyone else I know. If I didn't, perhaps my feeling about Felix wouldn't be quite so strong. And I'll try to curb my tongue when I speak about him to you."

Penelope had begun to feel much wearied by the interview, with its demands upon her emotional strength and the strange, tingling excitement with which Gordon's presence wrought upon her nerves, just as it had done at their previous meeting.

His compelling personality, that had burst so unexpectedly and so intimately into her life, inspired in her the wish to believe in him. But his bitterness toward her brother, notwithstanding their evident intimacy, made her hesitate. He seemed so sincere and so straightforward that her impulse was to meet him with equal frankness. But she was still a little doubtful, a little fearful.

She felt that she must know more about the mysterious relation, with its apparent contradictions, between him and Felix before she could give him the confidence he seemed to desire.

"It is all very strange," she said, "and after you are gone I shall wonder whether I have been dreaming or whether some one named 'Hugh Gordon' has really been here saying such bitter things about my brother. Does he know that you have such a poor opinion of him?"

"Does he know it?" Gordon exclaimed, facing her impulsively and speaking with emphasis. "Indeed he does! He knows just how much I—but there! I promised to bridle my tongue. Well, he has had a great deal more information upon that head than you have!"

"Well, then, I'll have to forgive you the hard things you've said about him to me, since you've been just as frank with him first!"

"Thank you! But you know they are all true, Penelope!"

She drew back, a little offended that he should insist a second time upon this point, and there was a touch of scornfulness in her tones as she rejoined with dignity:

"I do not deny that my brother has faults, but is that any reason why I should discuss them with a stranger?"

"Don't say that, Penelope!"

His cry came so straightly and so simply from his heart that its honest feeling and the look of pain upon his face moved her to quick contrition and to warmer confidence. Surely, she told herself, there could be no doubting his ardent friendliness toward her mother and herself, whatever might be his attitude toward Felix.

"I have known about you such a long time," he was hurrying on in pleading speech, "that you are like an old friend—no, more than that, like a sister in my thought of you, and I want you to feel that way toward me. It may seem strange to you, Penelope, but it is true, that you and your mother are nearer and dearer to me than any one else in the world. That's why it hurts when you call me a stranger, although I know I can hardly seem more than that to you, as yet."

He sat down beside her and took one of her hands for a moment in both of his. "But we are going to change that, if you'll let me," he said, a smile lighting his serious face. "If you'll let me I'm going to be a genuine sort of brother to you. I haven't the genius that Felix has, I'll never create anything beautiful or wonderful, but I have got a knack for business and I can make money. I don't care anything about money for itself, but I do care a lot for all the things one can do with it.

"My head is full of ideas and plans for using the money I shall make as a lever for helping the world along. I know such things interest you, Penelope. You like to read and think about them and I'm sure you'd have done great work in that line if—if Felix—if there had been no accident. And if you will give me the benefit of your reading and thinking, it will help me in the working out of my plans."

"I? Could I be of any use? When I am such a prisoner and have so little strength? I've only read and thought a little—I don't know anything as people do who come face to face with actual conditions. But you don't know," and a sharp, indrawn breath and the wistfulness of her eyes told him how much she was moved by his proposal, "you don't know what it would mean to me!"

"I can guess, Penelope—sister—you don't mind if I call you that? I know a little, and your face tells me a good deal more, about how your spirit has rebelled and how you have battled with it and won the victory. You haven't found it easy to be a prisoner in a wheel-chair!"

"Indeed, I have not!"

She bent her thin, humped and crooked body forward with fresh energy and a spark of the spirit she had conquered flashed out again in her dark eyes and tired face.

"My soul has longed so to do something, to be something, to be able to use my abilities and my energies as other people do! I have longed so fiercely to go about and see the beautiful and wonderful things in the world, to achieve something myself and to meet as an equal other people who have done things worth while! If there is hell anywhere it used to be in my heart! I fought it—it was the only thing there was to do—by myself, for I couldn't add to mother's troubles such a burden as that would have been. Father knew, a little, of how I felt, before he died. But afterwards I fought it out myself—it took years to do it—and at last forced myself into a sort of content, or resignation.

"I know I am some comfort to mother, although I have cost her so much care. But for a long time her chief pleasure, after her delight in Felix, has been in our companionship. So that is something, and I read a good deal and think all I can, and I try to do through others the little good in the outside world that is possible to me."

She leaned back again feebly and closed her eyes for a moment in physical weariness. "And so at last," she went on, meeting his compassionate look with a faint smile, "I come to be—not unhappy."

"And now the opportunity is coming," he assured her impulsively, "for you to make some use of your sweet, strong spirit and your capable brain. But I don't know—Felix—I don't know—" he hesitated, casting at her a keen, inquiring glance, but continued in a confident tone: "But you'll understand, you'll see it's for the best! Oh, I know you'll agree that I'm doing the right thing!"

He saw the fatigue in her countenance and rose to go. "I'm afraid I've tired you, Penelope, but I hope you'll forgive me when I tell you what pleasure our talk has given me. Before I go I want to ask you one more thing—about your mother. Did she—was she much grieved by what I did about—Felix and that bribery business?"

A look of gratification crossed Penelope's face. "I hoped you wouldn't go away without saying something about that," she said frankly. "Of course, it grieved her. She was deeply hurt."

"I knew she would be," he interrupted sorrowfully. "But it was the best way I could see. I thought it would be a warning to Felix."

"Of course she didn't believe it was true. She thought you were acting under a conviction of public duty and that you were mistaken in your understanding of what had happened. You impressed her very much when you were here and she thought so much about you afterwards that it was hard for her to reconcile your action with your friendship for Felix. But she did and finally came to think it really noble in you to hold what you thought to be the public good above your personal feelings."

"But it was Felix I was thinking of chiefly," he protested. "Still, it was very sweet of her, and very like her, too, to look at it in that way. Would she—do you think she would be glad to see me if she were at home?"

"I am sure she would," replied Penelope cordially. "She was so pleased with her fancy of your being her dream son and of your coming toward us out of the snow-storm like some one in a dream— dear mother! It all pleased her so much! And she talked much and tenderly about you afterwards. But there was something that disturbed her, and I must tell you about it, for she will want to know if I explained it to you."

She stopped a moment and threw an observant glance upon her listener. Absorbed in what she was saying, he was looking at her with his keen eyes and serious face all soft and tender with emotion.

Penelope felt her heart yearn toward him with entire trust. "Felix has never cared for us as much as this man does already," she thought.

"Mother was afraid," she continued, "that you might think, from what she said about her hopes when Felix was a little boy, that she is dissatisfied with him now. Of course, you know that isn't true. I've told you enough for you to see how she delights and glories in him. She would have liked, I think, to see him become a great preacher or a great reformer. But his bent wasn't that way, and I don't believe that if he had been either she could have been prouder of him than she is now."

"Well, I can never be a great preacher, or a great reformer either, or, indeed, a great anything. But I hope I shall be able to do some good in the world, in little spots here and there, and I want very much to bring more happiness into her life and yours. I would like to be to her a son. But—I don't know——"

He hesitated again and Penelope saw doubt come into his face and his eyes grow wistful.

"No, I don't know how it will be. I can do it—" Again he stopped for a moment and, gazing into the distance as he went on, he seemed to Penelope to be speaking more to himself than to her. "I can do it only by giving to you and to her, to her especially, very great sorrow first. Sometimes, I'm not quite sure——"

Then sudden resolution seemed to seize him. His lips shut and his figure stiffened with determination. "But it has to be—it has to be," he declared abruptly. His air was forceful to the verge of aggressiveness as he turned to her again.

"Good-bye, Penelope. Give my love to your mother and tell her I was sorry not to see her. It has been good to see you once more and to have this talk with you. I shall come again some time if you will let me. But I shall not believe you unwilling to see me unless you yourself tell me so."

"You are a strange man," she replied, looking at him with frank curiosity but entire friendliness, "and you interest me very much. Whenever you wish to come again you may be sure that no matter what you may have been doing, I at least shall be glad to see you."

His abrupt, aggressive manner softened, and a pleading note sounded in his voice as he replied:

"Anyway, you'll try to think, won't you, that I believe, from the bottom of my heart, that what I am doing and shall do concerning Felix is for the good of everybody, even for his good, too, extraordinary as that may seem. That's the most I can say, until the time comes for me to tell you the whole story. But you shall know it sometime, Penelope. Good-bye."

CHAPTER XII

DR. ANNISTER HAS DOUBTS

Early in the second week of Brand's absence his secretary had another call from Hugh Gordon. Henrietta was aware of a little thrill of pleasure when the office boy brought her his card, and quickly accounted for it to herself by thinking that perhaps he would have some news of her employer. But he had nothing to tell her and he made excuse for coming by asking if Brand had returned or if she had heard from him.

Henrietta was puzzled by his manner as he made this inquiry. For he showed no anxiety, and when she replied he received her answer with as little interest as if he had known beforehand what she would say.

"I hoped you would be able to tell me something about him," she added.

"I do not know where he is," he replied, "but I am positive that you have no occasion to feel anxious about him. I am quite sure he will return, perhaps before long. I assure you, if anything should happen to him, I should know it before any one else."

He spoke with such sincerity that her lingering distrust faded away, while his abundant physical vigor, manifest alike in his appearance and his manner, made a strong appeal to her feminine nature. He seemed so full of energetic purpose, and he looked at her with such a self-assured, straightforward gaze that she could no longer withhold the confidence she felt him to be demanding. Nor did the fact that her woman's instinct, quickly discovering the scarcely concealed admiration in his eyes and countenance, told her the reason for his visit lessen her inclination to give him the trust he desired.

"Do you think," she anxiously asked, "that I ought to report Mr. Brand's disappearance to the police?"

"No," he said with abrupt positiveness, "I do not."

Then he seemed to take second thought and purposely to soften his manner as he proceeded: "When he returns do you think he would be pleased to learn that another hullaballoo had been made over his absence, doubtless on necessary business?"

"Oh, no, I am sure he would not! He didn't like it at all the other time. It was only—I feel so much responsibility—and I am so uncertain as to what I ought to do. I am not letting anybody know"—she hesitated and blushed—"except you, that I don't really know where he is. I thought it was what he would wish if—if he is on a business trip—in West Virginia—or anywhere. But if anything has happened—should happen—to him——"

"Don't feel anxious on that score. I shall be the first one to know if any harm comes to him, and I give you my word that you shall be informed as soon as possible. I came in to give you this assurance, as I feared you would be worried by his long absence."

Henrietta was surprised when her visitor left to find that their conversation had lasted for half an hour. "It didn't seem so long," she thought, smiling in the pleasant glow that still enveloped her consciousness.

"I hope I didn't say anything I ought not," her thought ran on, with just a tinge of anxiety. "He is such a compelling sort of man, you have to trust him, and he's so blunt and direct himself that before you know it you are being just as frank as he is."

She reviewed their talk and reassured herself, with much gratification, that nowhere had it touched what the most sensitive loyalty to her employer could have thought forbidden ground.

"It's very curious," she marvelled, "how he knows about Mr. Brand's affairs. They must be the very closest friends or he could never know so much about Mr. Brand's ambitions and how he feels about his art. And yet there was a flash in his eyes every time Mr. Brand's name was mentioned, and he looked just as if he were trying to control an angry feeling. Still, they are surely friends.... His mustache is very handsome. I wonder why he doesn't let it grow longer."

Toward the end of the week he came again and renewed his assurances of Brand's safety, and again they talked happily together for a length of time that startled Henrietta when she looked at her watch after he left. Her confidence in him increased with each interview and so also did her puzzlement as to his relations with Felix Brand. For several days she debated with herself as to what she ought to do and at last, in her anxiety and doubt, she sought the counsel of Dr. Annister.

She told him the whole story, admitting that she did not herself believe the architect had taken the southern trip, giving her reasons for that suspicion, describing the three visits of Hugh Gordon and recounting the assurances he had made her of Brand's safety and early return.

"I haven't come to you before, Dr. Annister," she said, "because I didn't like to worry you about it. I know what a nervous condition Mildred is in, anyway, because she doesn't hear from him and I thought that if she guessed the real state of affairs it would be ten times harder for her."

"I fear Mildred will have a nervous collapse if he does not return soon," said Dr. Annister gravely, "or we do not get some assurance that all is well with him. You say that this Hugh Gordon declares he doesn't know where Felix is?"

"Yes, that is what he says, but at the same time he seems so confident there can be nothing wrong that when I talk with him I feel it will be all right. And then afterwards I wonder if I am doing the right thing in keeping it all so quiet. Do you think, Dr. Annister, that we ought to put the case into the hands of the detectives? You know, if we did that and then he should come back in a few days, as he did before, he would be dreadfully annoyed."

Dr. Annister, in a shabby leather arm-chair, in whose roomy depths his undersized figure seemed smaller than ever, leaned forward with his elbows on its arms and thoughtfully struck together the ends of his fingers.

They were in his private office, where this chair had been for twenty years his favorite seat. It was his attitude and gesture of deepest abstraction. Many a time, sitting thus, and gazing with intent eyes on nothing at all, had he found light on difficult cases. And many a nervous wreck among his patients had marched back to health and vigor to the rhythmic tapping of those finger-ends.

Just now he was considering the possibility that Felix Brand, the famous young architect, his son-in-law to be, might have sunk out of sight intentionally in order to indulge in deeply hidden debauch. Although it had but recently become manifest, that suggestion of sensuality in the young man's refined and handsome countenance, the physician's only ground of objection to the early marriage for which his daughter and her lover had pleaded, had grown stronger of late. But if Brand should be found in some low dive it might get out and the carrion-loving sensational newspapers would make an ill-smelling scandal into which Mildred's name would be dragged. No, if that were the explanation, it would be better to let him return in his own good time and then have a serious talk with him and try to get at the truth.

"No," he said at last, taking down his arms and leaning back into the chair's capacious embrace, "I don't think we'd better take that extreme measure; at least, not yet. In my judgment you've acted prudently, my dear, in not letting anybody know his absence is other than an ordinary business matter. It is now about two weeks since he—went away?"

"Two weeks and a half."

"Well, I think we'd better wait at least another week before we do anything. And, meantime, all that you've told me will be a secret between you and me."

"Thank you, Dr. Annister. You've relieved my anxiety very much, indeed. And I'm so glad you think as you do, for I dreaded doing anything about it for fear it might get into the papers and there'd be all that horrid publicity and the reporters coming and catechizing me every day."

"Wait a bit," he said as she rose to go. "I want to ask you more about this Gordon. He seems to you an honest, straightforward sort of man?"

"Oh, entirely, Dr. Annister! He is so frank and sincere and direct that you can't help believing in him. He seems to know Mr. Brand very, very intimately, too. And yet such an angry look crosses his face sometimes when we speak about Mr. Brand that I am very much puzzled. It doesn't seem as if they could be such good friends as they would have to be for Mr. Gordon to know all he does."

"I wish I could see him and talk with him myself. Do you know his address?"

"No, sir. And he's not in either the telephone or the city directory."

"Well, if he comes to your office again ask him to come up here with you. Explain how anxious we are—doubtless he knows that Felix and Mildred are engaged—and say that it would be a great relief to us if we could hear from his own lips that he is still sure of Mr. Brand's safety. I'll see him first and if he inspires my confidence as he does yours I'll have Mildred come in and talk with him, too. Won't you go up and see Mildred and Mrs. Annister?"

"I'd love to, Dr. Annister, but—Mildred will be so anxious for news, and I can't tell her anything more than I have a dozen times already, and——"

"I understand," he interrupted. "I know, it's hard not to be able to tell her what she longs to hear. Ah, Henrietta," and he shook his head sadly, "there isn't a man on the face of this earth that is worthy of such a wealth of love! But how are the mother and sister? And how is the mortgage getting on?"

He was standing in front of her, and, although she was not a tall woman, their eyes were on a level. His deeply lined, thin face was so pale, that, with its white mustache, heavy, gray-white eyebrows and crown of silver-white hair, it was like an artist's study of white against white.

As Henrietta looked into it a sudden vision came to her of the long procession of men and women who had passed through that office, stricken and fearful, their desperate eyes pleading with that one pale face for help, and a lump came in her throat. She coughed before she could speak.

"We begin to think mother is getting better," she said, "now that she is feeling so much at ease about money matters. And the mortgage is slowly dwindling. If I have no bad luck I expect to clear it all off by the end of the summer."

"Good! You are a splendid, plucky girl, my dear, and I'm as proud of you as your father would have been!"

CHAPTER XIII

MILDRED IS MILITANT

The next afternoon Henrietta left her office early, in order to discharge some commissions for her sister in the shopping district. Stopping to look at a window display of spring costumes, her eye was caught by a dress that suited her taste exactly. She inspected it from both sides and went into the doorway that she might get the back view.

"What a lovely suit and how becoming it would be for me!" she thought. "I wonder if I could afford to buy it. Oh dear, no! I mustn't even think of such a thing! It would be just that much off the mortgage payments."

She turned away with a sigh and found herself face to face with Hugh Gordon, who glanced with a quizzical smile from her to the window.

"Did you hear one of the commandments cracking?" she laughed. "I've just been coveting one of those suits as hard as I could."

"Are you going in to buy it now?" he asked with a suggestion of disappointment in his air, as if, having come upon her so unexpectedly, he disliked to lose her again at once.

"Oh, dear, no! I'm not going to buy it at all. I can't afford it."

"Well, then, you are wise not to buy it, and the best way is not even to think about it any more," he said in that abrupt manner to which, although it had sometimes startled her at their first meetings, she had already grown accustomed. She had told herself more than once, indeed, that she liked it in him, it seemed so expressive of his masculine forcefulness and decision of character.

"How different you are from Mr. Brand," she answered smiling. "He would say in such case, 'If you want it why don't you buy it at once? There's no time like the present for doing the things you want to do.'"

His brows came together in a quick frown and his eyes flashed as he said: "Yes, I know that is his philosophy of life. But it's not mine by a long ways. I think it despicable."

His voice sounded harsh and angry and Henrietta looked up in surprise at the intensity of feeling it betrayed.

Then she remembered Dr. Annister's suggestion and exclaimed, "Oh, by the way, I've a message for you!"

He listened with interest as she told him of Dr. Annister's desire to see him and asked if he could either go there with her now or make an appointment for another day.

"It would be kind of you to go," she added. "You have relieved my mind so much about Mr. Brand that I am hoping you can make them feel a little less anxious, too—especially Miss Annister. I suppose you know she and Mr. Brand are engaged!"

"Yes, I know it," he answered curtly as he looked at his watch. "I have some leisure time now, a couple of hours, and I can go at once as well as not. I don't know," he went on doubtfully, "whether or not Miss Annister will want to see me. She is much prejudiced against me."

Henrietta's mind flew back to the decided opinions Mildred had advanced to the reporters, which, however, she was glad to remember, they had modified in their accounts.

"She was, some weeks ago," Henrietta began reassuringly.

"And is yet," he declared. "I happen to know that her feeling toward me is very hostile. And Felix has encouraged her in it."

"She is so very much in love with Mr. Brand and so wildly anxious it would be a great kindness to give her even a little comfort," Henrietta gently urged.

"I'll do what I can," he replied after a moment's hesitation. He spoke slowly and his companion, looking up, wondered at the extremely serious expression that had come into his face.

As they entered the Annister home, Mildred and her mother were descending the stairs, dressed for the street. Henrietta looked up from the doorway and saw Mildred's countenance transfigured with sudden joy.

The girl sprang down the steps with a cry of "Oh, Felix, Felix!" Gordon stepped in from the vestibule where his features had been blurred by the brilliant sunlight behind him, and Mildred, stricken with disappointment, threw up her hands to cover the tears she could not control, and sobbing, rushed back up the stairs. Gordon looked grimly on, his face set and scowling, as if he were gripping deep into his very soul with an iron determination.

"Come up to the drawing-room," said Mrs. Annister, when Henrietta had presented her companion and explained their errand, "and I'll send for Dr. Annister."

Thither also she presently brought Mildred. But the stately air with which the girl entered the room and the haughty inclination of her head with which she acknowledged Gordon's greeting told how little trust she expected to feel in anything he might say.

In answer to Dr. Annister's inquiries Gordon told them, in substance, what he had already said to Henrietta and gave them, in brief, curt sentences, that seemed to spring spontaneously out of the force and simplicity of his character, the same assurances that Brand was in no danger and that he would return, safe and well, in his own good time.

"That," he added, "is all that I can tell you, because it is all I know. But I do know that."

"Father!" cried Mildred, springing from her chair, her slender figure militantly erect, her eyes flashing and her voice thrilling with indignation. "How can you sit there and listen to this man's talk! Why don't you throttle him and make him tell all he knows? It's plain enough that if he knows this much he must know where Felix is and why he doesn't write to me. But I see through it all! He's got Felix locked up somewhere, perhaps in some mountain cabin in West Virginia, or perhaps he's killed him. He ought to be arrested! If you don't care enough for Felix to have it done I'll telephone for the police at once and he shall not leave this house until they come!"

Her words poured forth in an angry torrent, and then, with a sobbing cry, she swept from the room. Dr. Annister leaped to his feet as if to follow her, then turned with a hand outstretched to his wife.

"You'd better go to her," he said anxiously. "She's hysterical and must be put to bed. I'll be there presently. I hope you will pardon my daughter's outburst," he added, turning to Gordon with a little bow. "She is overwrought from having brooded over this matter much more than it deserves. I don't share her suspicion of you and you seem to me to show every mark of a man speaking honestly what he believes to be the truth. But you will pardon me if I say I do not quite understand how it can all be true."

They had all risen and Gordon was looking straight down into the little physician's eyes with an expression so serious and solemn that Henrietta caught her breath, intently listening for what he was about to say.

"No," he replied, slowly, gravely, "I do not wonder that you do not understand. Neither do I."

Professional inquiry was in the keen glance with which Dr. Annister searched for an instant his visitor's face and eyes. Henrietta, watching him, guessed that he was probing for some sign of mental aberration. But apparently he was satisfied on that score, for as he followed them out he gave her a reassuring pat upon the arm.

"Well," he said more cheerfully, "since this is all you can tell us, we shall have to wait with what patience we can for Mr. Brand's return. But I will tell you frankly, Mr. Gordon, that I, at least, have confidence in you and accept your assurances."

He did not tell them, however, by what course of reasoning he had quickly come to this conclusion. That was something to be kept closely locked in his own breast until he should see Felix Brand again. For he had decided that the most probable key to the mystery was that his daughter's betrothed was indulging in some secret form of debauchery, perhaps solitary drunkenness, perhaps indulgence in some drug, perhaps mere beastliness, and that this fact was known to his intimate friend, Hugh Gordon, who, in single-minded loyalty, was trying to protect him. A normal man's disgust at such a course of conduct, thought the doctor, would explain the antipathy which he was often unable to conceal when Brand's name was mentioned.

Henrietta thought her companion somewhat abstracted on their way down town, and unusually serious, even for him, who was accustomed to take, as she had already learned, a serious view of himself and the world. He crossed the ferry with her, and not until they had ensconced themselves in a quiet corner of the boat's upper deck did he seem to settle the question which had been disturbing his mind. But settled she decided it must be, for he now gave himself up to enjoyment of her society.

When they landed he walked with her to her trolley car, where they stood, still talking, until the motorman began making preparations to start.

"Good-bye," he said unsmilingly, as he held out his hand. "I shall see you again sometime, but I fear it will not be soon."

CHAPTER XIV

"THERE IS NOT ROOM FOR US BOTH"

"What shall I do?" Henrietta Marne exclaimed aloud as she looked despairingly at the papers that littered her desk. "Here are half a dozen letters, this morning, that ought to have his immediate attention, to say nothing of all the others that I've got stacked away in this drawer. Well, I'll just have to keep on as I've done before and answer them in my own name, saying that Mr. Brand is temporarily out of the city and as soon as he returns, etc. If he doesn't come back soon," she grumbled on as she seated herself at the typewriter, "I'll be as hysterical as Mildred is, though I'm not in love with him."

She did what she could with the morning's mail, looking at one envelope as she carefully put it away unopened, with more than a little interest and curiosity, as she saw on its upper corner the firm name of "Gordon and Rotherley." After she had finished the letter writing she busied herself for an hour with such duties as it was possible for her to take up.

The architect's suite of offices was on an upper floor of a high building and from its windows one's vision soared far over the city southward and westward. Henrietta paused now and then in the course of her work to forget her anxieties in the sights and thoughts that greeted her in that wide view. Down below, at the bottom of the street canyons, people and vehicles were rushing back and forth.

But her eyes never rested long upon them. Rather, they traveled slowly out over the mighty plain of roofs, broken by chimneys and spires, by great, square buttes of buildings, by domes, turrets and towers, across the bay, gleaming silver-white or glowing copper-red in the sun, on to where the swelling hills of Staten Island loomed dimly against the horizon.

In the brilliant sunshine a thousand plumes of cloud-white steam waved gaily above the castellated plain of roofs and shook out their tendrils in the breeze. "Peace pipes" Henrietta sometimes called them to herself, as she thought of all that their fragile beauty, forever dissolving and forever being renewed, meant to the city beneath them. She liked to think of them, as she watched them curling and waving upward toward the blue, as a sign and compact of earth's peace and good-will.

Her bent of mind was much more practical than imaginative, but she could never look out over this scene without feeling her nerves thrill with vague consciousness of the titanic energies ceaselessly grinding, striving, achieving, beneath that surface of roofs and towers. And now, as always when she stopped to gaze from her window for a few moments, she felt her own pulses quicken in response and her own inward being stir, as if those waving white plumes were trumpet calls to activity.

She turned from the window, more restless than before, impatient with the necessity of merely sitting there and waiting. In Brand's private room the books she had got for him three weeks before still lay ranged upon his desk, in readiness for his return at any moment. In her spare hours she had been reading some of them herself and now she went to get one as the best way in which to put in her time. As she brought it back to her own room her thoughts, as they did a hundred times a day, hovered over and around her various speculations concerning the mystery of her employer's absence.

"I wonder," they presently ran, "if it could be possible that he is hiding somewhere in the city just to indulge in some sort of orgy." And this time denial of such a possibility did not, as formerly, spring up spontaneously in her mind. "I don't like to think he could be that sort of a man," she temporized with her budding doubt, "for he always seems so refined and thoroughly nice, and he's always been such a perfect gentleman to me. But it's evident that Mr. Gordon, who knows him so well, hasn't a very high opinion of him, except in his art."

The telephone broke in upon her musing, and as she put the receiver to her ear and said "hello" she was almost as much astonished as delighted to hear in reply the voice of Felix Brand himself. He told her that he had just got home, after another beastly trip into the back woods of West Virginia, where he had had an accident. He had slipped and sprained his ankle—no, it was nothing serious, and was all right now, but it had kept him a prisoner for nearly two weeks in a mountain cabin a thousand miles from anywhere, and he would be at the office as soon as he had had his luncheon.

Glad as she was that he was there once more to take up the matters that needed his attention so badly, Henrietta was almost afraid to face him, when she heard his voice in the outer room, lest there might be that in his appearance which would give form and force to the doubts that were stirring in her mind.

But he seemed no different from his usual, affable and well-dressed self. He wore, in all seasons, very dark or black clothing, which was always in perfect condition, and fitted his well-proportioned figure trimly and closely rather than with the looser English cut. His dark eyes looked down upon her with their usual caressing smile and his clean-shaven face, with its finely modeled, regular features, was as handsome, as refined, as ever.

But, no,—his secretary was conscious of something in its expression she had never noticed there before. What with the rejoicing that filled her heart and the work that kept her hands and brain busy all the rest of the day, she had not time to think what it was, or to give it any definite form in her thoughts, until her homeward trip by subway, ferry and trolley gave her leisure to scan closely the happenings of the afternoon.

Even then she merely said to herself that there was something in his face and eyes that did not seem quite like him, something that was not so "nice" as he had always seemed to be. She did not know enough about the evil undercurrents of life to give the thing more specific definition. But she did know that, whatever it was, it stirred, deep within her, a faint sense of repulsion.

"Did you get my letter?" was one of the first things he said to her.

"No, Mr. Brand, I've heard nothing at all from you since you left."

"You didn't? That's queer. I gave it to the porter to mail and he probably forgot all about it. I went away so hurriedly I didn't have time to write until after I got aboard the train. There were some directions in it about the work here. Well, we'll have to go back and take things up where we left off. And the first thing is that letter I wrote and asked you not to send. Where is it?"

"Oh, I ventured to mail that—I knew how important it was, and I found out enough about the business to feel sure you would want me to."

"You did! How fortunate!"

"Then it was all right? I am so glad! But I don't deserve all the credit. Your friend, Mr. Hugh Gordon, was here— —"

"What! That fellow? Did he dare to come here?"

The start, the sudden turn, the sharp exclamation with which Brand broke into her sentence were so different from his habitual manner of deliberate movement and courteous speech that Henrietta gazed at him in amazement. Surprise and indignation sat upon his countenance.

"Why, yes," she faltered. "He was here several times. The first time, a few days after you left, he told me he knew you wanted that letter sent."

She went on to repeat what Gordon had told her and ended with: "Of course, I didn't take his word for it entirely, but after what he told me I was able to find out enough to make me feel sure it was the right thing to do."

"You did quite right," he told her cordially. "But I am surprised to learn of his doing, for me, a friendly act like that. You said he was here afterwards?"

"Yes, several times. He came to tell me that you were quite safe and well and would return before long. I was very glad to have the assurance, for, of course, I couldn't help being anxious."

He opened his mouth as if to speak, closed it again suddenly, then, as he busied his hands with some papers on his desk, took sudden resolution and, though his face paled, said in a casual way:

"Did he tell you where I was?"

"He said he didn't know where you were, but that he did know positively that if anything should happen to you he would be the first person to know anything about it. I felt so much less anxious after that."

"Yes, it was quite true, what he said," Brand assented slowly. He hesitated again, as if on the verge of farther speech, and Henrietta waited. After a moment he turned to her a face out of which he seemed purposely to have forced all expression and asked:

"How did he impress you? Do you think he looks like me? Some people say he does."

"Oh, he impressed me very favorably, indeed. He seemed so sincere and so kind and so much in earnest. No, I didn't think he looked like you, except in a general way. His features, perhaps, are something like yours, but he himself is so different, his manner, his expression—everything."

She spoke interestedly, the color rising in her cheeks, and Brand watched her narrowly. "Oh, that reminds me," she exclaimed, "there's a letter for you from him. It's in my desk."

She went to get it and as her employer's gaze followed her his eyes widened and his face grew ashen. "My God!" he muttered, and there was consternation in his whispered tone. Then sudden anger flashed over him. Henrietta felt it quivering in his tones as he said, when she gave him the envelope:

"Thank you, Miss Marne. You did just right about mailing that letter, and I am much pleased that you did. But hereafter don't trust that fellow Gordon in any way. For all his pretense of friendship, he is the worst enemy I have and would stop at nothing to injure me. Hereafter he must not be allowed to enter these rooms. Will you please tell the boy that these are my orders—that Hugh Gordon must be put out at once if he attempts to come inside my door again."

Henrietta noticed that the architect took the letter she gave him with a hand that trembled slightly, cast at it a single frowning, hostile glance and hastily but carefully put it away in his breast pocket. She remembered that just so had he looked at the previous letter from Gordon, and with just the same angry care had put it away unopened.

In that inner pocket it remained untouched, just as had the former one, by turns searing his very heart with impotent anger and chilling it with fear, until a late hour of the night, when he sat alone before his library fire. Then, at last, with the look and manner of a man forced to touch a loathed object, he took it out and opened it.

"Felix Brand, I have come to a decision," the letter abruptly began. "It must be either you or I. Until lately I thought there might be room for us both. But there isn't. If you had paid any attention to what I told you before, had shown any remorse for the evil you have done, or any intention of reforming your conduct, I might have come to a different conclusion. I will say more than that. If you had felt in your soul the desire to get yourself together and be a real man instead of a source of pollution, and had shown in your thoughts and actions the willingness and the ability to try to make yourself over, I would have recognized your right to live.

"In that case, I would have gone, perhaps not willingly, but feeling it right to go, back to where I came from, and I would have let you alone. At least, I would have tried to do that, because I give you full credit for your genius, of which I have none, and know its value to the world. But I might not have succeeded. For I have tasted life and found it good and the desire to live, the will to live, is so strong within me that it might have been stronger than the sense of my duty, of your right, or anything else.

"But it is useless to speculate about that, because you grow worse instead of better. You are like one of those people who, apparently unharmed themselves, carry about with them the germs of typhoid and scatter destruction wherever they go. The sooner the world is rid of you the better for it, and the better for you, too.

"You will be surprised, and probably angry, to hear from your secretary that I have visited your office. I went, primarily, because I wanted to meet Miss Marne, but also because I knew she ought to mail that letter and, finally, because I wanted to reassure her about your absence and prevent any measures being taken to search for you. The first reason is none of your affair and on the other two counts you ought to be grateful to me, though I don't suppose you will be. I took some trouble to find out about the matters on which that letter bore, because I knew how important you considered them. You may find it difficult to believe, but it is true that, although I despise and loathe you, I did not wish to be responsible for such smash-up of your plans as longer delay in the sending of your letter would have caused. The bond between us is too close, Felix Brand, for me not to feel compassion for you sometimes.

"I could have kept you away longer this time if I had not felt sorry for Miss Annister. It was on her account that I let you return when I did. Don't make her suffer that way again. If you don't give her beforehand some sort of plausible preparation for your next absence—for there will be another, and that before long—I shall enable her father to find out some plain truths about you that may complicate matters for you in that quarter.

"My mind is made up, Felix Brand. There is not room in the world for both you and me. I shall try not to hurt you publicly again, because it does no good. And efficient measures are the only ones that appeal to me. But I am going to do my best to push you off the edge for good and all. I have doubted and hesitated and argued the matter over and over with myself and tried to see some way of compromise. But you will not come my way and I loathe yours. And you know quite well that you yourself are responsible for the whole business, even for the fate that awaits you. You will merely suffer the consequences of your own actions. For I believe I shall win. I know that you will put up a good fight, for we have fought before, and, so far, you have won oftener than I have. But in the end, I shall win. I dare say you will think it impertinent in me to add that I am convinced it will be for your good, as well as for the world's benefit, that I should win. Nevertheless, I do think that very thing and so I can still declare myself,

"Yours sincerely,

"HUGH GORDON."

Felix Brand read this letter with an interest that made him, in spite of his abhorrence, go through it a second time before he lifted his eyes from its pages. For him its mysterious threats needed no explanation and as he sensed the full meaning of the fate it predicted, angry horror swept over him.

He shuddered as he glanced apprehensively about him, as though fearing to see take shape out of the air the intangible force with which, on that other night three weeks before, he had fought to the utmost of his strength, only to be overcome at last. The memory of that fierce struggle was upon him now, chilling his veins and clutching his heart with terror. And he would have to fight that invisible, relentless power over and over again to save himself from the black-magic destiny that threatened. Then, suddenly, fear and horror were swept away by a frenzy of rage that ramped through him all the more fiercely because there was nothing upon which it could wreak itself.

"You thief!" he cried, glaring about him with bloodshot eyes. "You hypocrite, to set yourself up as better than I am! Do you hear me? You hypocrite, thief, murderer!"

The exaltation of his anger gave him fresh strength and new confidence in himself and he tore the letter into bits and ground them beneath his heel as he shouted:

"This is what will happen to you! It's what you deserve and what you'll get, you damned thief!"

CHAPTER XV

FELIX BRAND HAS A BAD QUARTER OF AN HOUR

It was evident to Dr. Annister that Felix Brand was having a bad quarter of an hour. But the little physician, sitting upright in his capacious chair, his elbows on its arms and his finger-tips resting against one another, could not find it in his heart to abate in the least the penetrating gaze of his gray eyes or the gentle insistence of his questions. For the longer their talk continued the more he became convinced that the man before him was not speaking the truth and the more he felt it necessary, for his daughter's sake, to find out what was the truth.

"I am sorry to have to tell you, Felix," said Dr. Annister, in the beginning of their conversation, "that I am unable to feel entire confidence in your explanation of your long and mysterious absence."

The architect hesitated for a bare instant before he turned to reply. The other noted that he had to stop to think, that neither movement nor answer was spontaneous.

"Do you mean me to understand, Dr. Annister," he said courteously, "that you think I am lying?"

"Let's not put it just that way. Suppose we call it the endeavor on your part to conceal something you don't want known—the instinct of self-defense. Morally, doubtless, it is the same thing. But I am not concerned just now with the moral nature of the thing itself. I am much concerned, however, for Mildred's sake, with the nature of the thing behind it."

Brand shot a quick, uneasy glance at him and moved restlessly in his chair. But there was no change in the customary, soft modulations of his voice or the urbanity of his manner as he replied: "Pardon me, Dr. Annister, but you are taking for granted something you have no right to assume. You know that I am an honorable man, accustomed to show at least ordinary regard for the truth. And therefore I say that you have no right to doubt my word on mere suspicion."

"My suspicion, if you wish to call it so, is well enough grounded to deserve, on my part, the most careful attention and, on yours, entire respect. Your explanation seems to me to be so thin and full of holes as not to be worth a moment's notice. It would be puerile for me to tell you how many opportunities you would have had on the train, as you were leaving the railroad, when you returned to it, and on your way home, to write or to telegraph to me, to Mildred, or to Miss Marne, and give us some idea of your whereabouts and assurance of your safety."

"I did write, on the train, to Mildred and also to Miss Marne. Apparently, the letters were lost in the mails or the porter forgot to post them."

Dr. Annister's finger-tips patted one another softly while his eyes searched the patrician face of his companion and marked in it signs of uneasiness.

"I have always supposed," he said quietly, "that a telegraph line runs beside the railroad into West Virginia, and I have not heard that the wires were down during your absence."

Felix Brand rose and with hands thrust into his pockets moved uncertainly from one chair to another. "Mildred has entire confidence in my explanation," he said with a touch of defiance in his voice. "She knows I would not deceive her."

"Mildred is young," her father replied gently, "and ignorant of the evil of which there is such a plenty in the world. She is very, very much in love with her promised husband and if he told her that black is white the dazzle in her eyes would make her see it white. But, Felix, it is just because she is so young, so innocent and so much at the mercy of her loving heart that I must speak plainly to you. I don't expect you to be entirely worthy of such a wealth of pure young love as she gives you. The man doesn't live who is clean enough in heart and in life to be worthy of such a treasure. But I do expect you to be, Felix, and I must assure myself that you are, clean enough and honorable enough not to blight all the rest of her life. What is past is past, but from now on there must be nothing that will not bear the light of day."

Brand was moving slowly back and forth, his countenance expressive of inward debate and hesitation. He was asking himself if it would not be the wisest plan to lay his trouble frankly before the physician and ask for his help. But his pride and his confidence in himself drew back from such a step.

No, he told himself, nobody must know. It must be kept in the darkest secrecy—suppose the thing should get out, and into the papers! His heart quaked at the thought. And he could not feel sure what view Dr. Annister would take of the truth—he might forbid the marriage with Mildred. No, he would keep the truth locked in his own breast and fight his battle alone. Well, he was sure of winning. It might take a little time, but he had no doubt of the outcome. Nevertheless, there was some uncertainty in his manner, though his courteous tones were firm enough as he said:

"If you will not take my word—and permit me to say, Dr. Annister, that it has never been doubted before—what more can I say?"

"You can tell me the truth, Felix," bluntly replied his prospective father-in-law. "I am fond of you, my boy, very fond of you,—I think you know that. I am proud of your genius and I expect to see you become one of the most famous architects of our time. More than anything else in the world I want to see my little girl as happy, as your wife, as her love deserves she should be. But I must tell you frankly, Felix, that I am afraid. I am afraid for you and your future and very much afraid for that of my daughter with you. That's why I feel I must speak as plainly as I am going to. I wish you would make it easier for me by meeting me half way."

The architect, still moving about the room with slow restlessness, stopped short and cast a quick, suspicious glance at the physician. The sweat broke out on his forehead as the fear leaped into his heart that Dr. Annister had guessed the truth. He had to grope among his panic thoughts for a moment before he could reply. His voice was a little strained as he said:

"Meet you half way? I don't know what you mean?"

Dr. Annister leaned back in his chair and sighed. But his searching gray eyes did not leave the other's face nor fail to take note there of the frequent signs of inner perturbation. Sadly he was saying to himself that everything in Brand's expression and manner increased his fears and justified his suspicion.

"Well, then," he said, "let us come straight to the point. A look, an expression, a tell-tale sign that I don't like has been steadily growing stronger in your face for the last six months. For the physician, and especially for the one who deals as much as I do with the psychological results of misliving, a man's countenance becomes a veritable table of contents for the book of his life. And your face is beginning to tell me such a story of self-indulgence and sensuality as makes me unwilling to give my daughter to your arms."

Brand turned a little away, as if he would conceal the traitor face whose refined beauty this inquisitor was finding even less than skin deep. "Of course," he said, "I am not as innocent as I was a dozen years ago. But—what you would have, Dr. Annister? A saint? You know you would have to look far to find one among modern young men. I'm no worse than the most of them and much better than some."

The physician was leaning forward again in his chair, his finger-tips tapping. He paid no attention to his companion's defense but pursued his own line of thought with an increasing tensity in his voice.

"I have been watching that revealing table of contents in your face grow steadily plainer for the last six months. After each of these long absences, for which you can give no satisfactory explanation, the expression has become, to my eyes, stronger and more significant than before. It forces me to the hypothesis, almost to the conclusion, that you have been spending this time somewhere in the under-world, in some sort of secret debauch."

Brand wiped the starting beads of sweat from his brow, and said, "I don't believe you really think me that sort of man, Dr. Annister!"

"Or, possibly," the physician continued, "that you have become a victim to the alcohol or one of the drug habits. I don't see the signs of that sort of thing upon you, yet. But—well, if such is your misfortune, I wish, Felix, that you would confide in me. Such habits are curable and even if my other hypothesis, which your physical appearance has forced me to, should be true we might be able to find its cause in some nerve lesion susceptible of remedy. In either case, you know as well as I do, Felix, that there is disaster before you, physical, moral and mental, if you keep on. Make a clean breast of it, and I'll do my best to help you."

Again the temptation was assailing the architect's mind to accept this proffered help and shift his burden to the shoulders of this little but puissant man of healing. Perhaps those tapping fingers could make him whole again. But as he faced avowal of the truth his whole soul drew back. It was impossible—the one thing he could not do. Then came another idea, perhaps a way out.

"Suppose—I do not admit it, but suppose, for the sake of your argument, that your hypothesis should be true. What then—Mildred—what about— —"

Dr. Annister sprang to his feet and broke in upon the other's stumbling words in a voice whose low-toned intensity gave his listener an uncomfortable thrill: "Nothing could make me happier than to see my child the happy wife of the man she loves, if he deserves her love. But I'd rather see her dead than married to a man of gross and unclean life, who has made himself a slave to seasons of secret debauch!"

There was silence for a moment while Brand looked away, unwilling to meet the physician's eyes. His face was pale and he breathed as if there were a weight upon his chest. Again he was considering open confession. But when he spoke he said:

"Dr. Annister, you are most unjust. I told you the truth about my absence. On that question there is nothing more to be said. But it is my right to know, and I insist upon knowing, whether or not you have any basis whatever for these insinuations you have been making, except your own suspicions."

Mildred's father gazed thoughtfully at her betrothed for a moment before he replied. He was saying to himself that the man's words were candid enough in their import, but that, somehow, the speech had not rung true. There was no spark of indignation in those brown eyes, that seemed to have some difficulty in meeting his. Nor was there any quiver of that honest resentfulness he longed to see. Beneath Brand's habitual manner of slightly ceremonious politeness and deference he discerned uncertainty of thought and purpose.

"There's something wrong here," the physician was thinking, "something woefully wrong. He doesn't seem to feel the monstrosity of what I've almost been charging him with." Unconsciously he shook his head sadly as he began to speak aloud:

"As I told you before, Felix, with the knowledge I have spent a lifetime of hard work gaining, I don't need any better evidence than my own eyes can give. I consider it as worthy of confidence as any information I might have from another. That and my own intelligence are the sole ground of my fears. These did have, however, some slight corroboration in the rather mysterious manner and assurances of your friend, Mr. Hugh Gordon."

At the sound of that name Brand faced sharply round upon the astonished doctor, anger flaming in his face and eyes.

"That man!" he cried. "Are you taking his word against mine? He is my worst enemy, and he will stop at nothing to injure me. He is a thief, a murderer, or would be if he dared. I demand that you tell me what he has been charging me with!"

Dr. Annister stared in amazement at this flare of hostility and wrath. "You mistake me, Felix," he said quietly, although inwardly he was wondering much as to the cause of the outburst. "I did not say he charged you with anything, nor did he. On the contrary, he seemed to me to be doing his best to execute a friendly office toward you. I thought it strange that he should be so positive you were in no danger of any sort and yet should not know where you were. He seemed sincere and straightforward and the only hypothesis upon which I could reconcile his two statements was one that strengthened what you call my suspicions."

While the doctor spoke Brand had been moving about with quick steps and sharp turns, scowling and muttering. "Oh, I know the fellow goes about making this pretense of friendship," he said sullenly, "but there's no trust to be put in him. He is bent on my ruin. But I'll get even with him, I'll down him yet!"

He took another turn or two, apparently endeavoring to get himself under control again, while Dr. Annister regarded him with gray brows wrinkled thoughtfully. He began to feel, uneasily, that there was more underneath this situation than he had guessed.

"Well, Felix," he said at last, "I am sorry that our conversation has had no better result. I hoped you would clear this matter up and, if you need help, would let me give you whatever advice and aid I could. Think the matter over more carefully and if you should see it in a different light come to me at any time and let me see what I can do for you."

"I thank you, Dr. Annister. I shall keep your kindness in mind, although I do not suppose I shall have any more occasion to make use of it in the future than I have now. But Mildred—" he hesitated as he turned an anxious countenance upon his companion. "You are not going to forbid our marriage on account of these baseless and unjust notions of yours?"

Down in his heart Dr. Annister was at that moment deciding that his daughter should never become this man's wife unless all his apprehensions and fears were first cleared away. But he feared the effect upon Mildred, especially at this juncture, of a forced breaking of the engagement. So he temporized.

"No, I shall not forbid it, or at least, not now. But I can not consent to a marriage in the early future, as you have both begged me to do. You will have to wait a while longer, Felix, and prove yourself worthy. I don't like these mysterious disappearances."

After Brand had gone the little doctor dropped down into his favorite arm-chair in his usual attitude of profound thought. "Poor Mildred! Poor little girl!" he was thinking. "I guess her mother had better take her abroad this summer and let us see if change and travel and absence won't have some effect on her devotion. It would be awfully lonely for me here, Mildred would be wretchedly unhappy and Margaret would have a devil of a time. Still, the experiment will be worth trying."

CHAPTER XVI

MRS. FENLOW IS ANGRY

"Harry, dear, do please conceal the newspaper in your handbag and carry it off with you," said Isabella Marne as her sister entered the dining room. The sun shone in upon a window full of blooming plants, a bowl of daffodils glowed upon the table and the whole room looked as cheerful and buoyant, as dainty and pleasing as did the little lady in a pink and white muslin gown who was putting the last touches to the breakfast table. "Mother is coming down this morning," she went on, "and I don't want her to see it."

"O, dear!" exclaimed Henrietta as she glanced at the head lines. "No, indeed, mother mustn't see this. It would worry her too much. Have you read it, Bella? Was he hurt?"

"The account says Mr. Brand wasn't hurt at all. But some of the others were—one rather badly, and Miss Andrews had her scalp cut. I hope it won't spoil her beauty."

"It must have been a narrow escape for them all," Henrietta commented in shocked tones as she glanced down the column. "Poor Mildred! She will be wild with anxiety and jealousy! You know, Bella, she can't bear for another woman to have a smile from him, or a little attention of any sort."

"Sh-h-h! Mother's coming! Do hide the paper quick and please talk real fast all through breakfast, so she won't think to ask for it until after you're gone. Mother would never, never let me go out with him in his auto again if she knew about this accident."

"I don't think you ought to, anyway, Bella. I wish you wouldn't."

"What harm does it do? And it gives me a little fun—about all I ever have, you know. Delia is having another season of introspection," she went on laughingly as Mrs. Marne entered the room and all three seated themselves at the table. "It has lasted two days already and I'm trembling with anxiety as to what will happen next. She was in such a brown study this morning that she would have sugared the eggs and salted the coffee if I hadn't been on the watch."

"Do you think she's making up her mind again to leave us?" said Mrs. Marne apprehensively.

"Oh, Delia's all right, except when she gets uneasy about the scarcity of matrimonial chances in this neighborhood. She doesn't really want to marry, at least not now, but she likes to think she could if she wanted to and she likes to see a new man once in a while, as she says, 'to pass a word with.' And I sympathize with her, even if I do have three letters a week from Warren."

"Bella!" exclaimed her mother, but with more amusement than reproof in her voice.

"You would, too, if you were twenty-five years younger," said Bella, leaning over to pat her mother's arm affectionately. "Anyway, I prove my sympathy with Delia by bringing to her all the stray crumbs of comfort I can find. I haven't told her yet—I'm waiting for her fit of introspection to reach the acute stage—but the grocer has got a new delivery boy, a nice young man, good-looking and polite. I wish somebody would be that kind to me!" she laughed, with a whimsical pout of her pretty lips. "Harry, if Mr. Brand says anything to you today about coming over here in his motor-car—" Henrietta looked up with a disapproving lift of her eyebrows and saw a sparkle of defiant mischief dancing in her sister's blue eyes—"just tell him, please," Bella proceeded with a toss of her head, "that my physician has ordered me to take an auto ride today as the only means of saving my life!"

It was mid-April and the very air thrilled with the hurry and promise of the spring that was making ready to leap at a single bound—would it be tomorrow, in three days, next week?—from swelling bud and bronzing tree into full flower and leafage. As Henrietta hastened down the street beneath budding trees busy at their yearly miracle and past little green lawns with their beds of crocuses and snowdrops and tulips, the splendid caressing sunshine bathed her in its gaiety, the smell of freshly turned earth challenged her to buoyant mood and the singing and fluttering and twittering of birds called her to equal delight in the radiant season. But all was not well with her world and she was more conscious of the anxiety in her heart than of the call of the spring that was storming at her senses.

True, she could begin to look forward now with reasonable surety, she told herself, to the last payment, in a very few months, upon their cottage with its little lawn and garden, and that would make sure, whatever might happen, a home for her mother. Bella would probably marry within a year the young physician to whom she had been engaged so long. They had waited for his graduation from the medical school of Harvard and now he wanted to be sure of a good enough practice to feel warranted in marrying. The delay had been necessary, too, on Bella's part, for her help in the care of their mother had been indispensable. But their improving financial prospects had acted like a magic draught upon Mrs. Marne and now, as she felt more and more assured of Henrietta's ability and success, she was rapidly growing so much better and stronger that she would soon be able to take care of their housekeeping and leave Bella free to marry as soon as her fiancé could offer her a home.

But Henrietta was so anxious about other things that these untangling perplexities gave her small comfort. Her sisterly caution told her it was not prudent for Isabella to go so frequently with Felix Brand in his automobile. Twice since Brand's return from his last absence had she found, when she reached home at the end of the day, that Bella had just returned from a long drive, wherein Brand's machine had apparently torn to tatters all speed laws and appeared to onlookers as a mere streak of color. After such a trip Bella's heightened spirits, Henrietta thought, made her very lovely and bewitching, with the flush in her cheeks, the sparkle in her eyes and her merry talk.

"She's young and gay-spirited and has so few pleasures," Henrietta thought, regardless of the fact that she herself was younger and had just as few, "that I feel awfully mean to object to anything that seems so innocent. But it is reckless of him to go so fast, and this accident last night—oh, I'm afraid it's dangerous. And then there's Mildred— if he was engaged to anybody else I shouldn't think anything about that; but—well, mother thinks it's all right and lovely of him to give Bella a little outing now and then; and if it wasn't I suppose he wouldn't do it."

But on this last point Henrietta was not without uneasiness. For little rifts were beginning to appear in that perfect confidence she had felt until recently in her employer. She had thought him the soul of uprightness and honor, but in his business affairs, nearly all of which passed through her hands, she knew that he had begun to make use of the barest falsehoods and to practice evasions and tricks that made her blush with shame to be the medium by which they were transmitted to paper.

Simple, sturdy forthrightness being the backbone of Henrietta's character, she could not help feeling as if she were an accomplice in his shiftiness and untruths when she typed and mailed his letters. She told herself that it was none of her affair, that she was no more than a machine in the work she did for him and that to look after her own morals was all that was incumbent upon her. Nevertheless, she was a good deal disturbed about it on this bright morning.

"He seems so different from what he was a few months ago," she thought with a sigh. "I don't understand why he should change so. I almost begin to feel like trying to find another situation. But I mustn't think about it now, for I can't afford yet to take any risks."

Her thoughts turned to another phase of Brand's character upon which also she was beginning to have doubts. She did not see many people, but a few bits of talk had reached her ears which made her wonder if the man whose character she had believed to be almost ideally fine and noble were not after all a devotee of sinister pleasures. She had begun to feel conscious, after his last return, of a feeling toward him of physical repulsion and this she knew was growing upon her. As she recalled these things her thoughts flashed uneasily back to her sister. She felt wretchedly ignorant and uncertain as to what she ought to do and wished there were some one better versed in worldly knowledge than herself to whom she could go for advice.

"I can't talk it over with mother," she thought, "because it would make her worry about it and about me, and I don't like to go to Dr. Annister, because he has enough troubles to listen to, with all those half-crazy patients of his, and Mrs. Annister admires Mr. Brand so much that she'd be offended by any suggestion that he isn't all right and—well, I don't think she's very level-headed anyway. I wish I could see Mr. Gordon again—it seems a long time. But I ought not to tell him anything about these things even if I should see him, since there seems to be so much feeling between him and Mr. Brand.

"And I'm afraid Bella wouldn't pay much attention to anything that was contrary to her own desires, anyway. I don't like the kind of influence Mr. Brand seems to be having over her. I understand it, because he used to make me feel that way myself—dissatisfied and selfish and wishful of all sorts of delightful things that I couldn't have. Well, I went through it all right, without any bad results except my own ugly feelings; and she's so dear and sweet and so happy-natured I guess she will, too, after a little."

She reached the avenue where ran the trolley line that carried her to the ferry and saw that she had just missed a car.

"Oh, dear! Isn't that provoking?" she muttered as she watched it rattling on its way. "And there isn't another one in sight yet. I hope I won't have to wait long, for I do want to get there early this morning, there's so much to do today."

Her thoughts sped on to her office and the duties that awaited her and hovered over the familiar figure of her employer at work at his desk.

"I don't see," she argued with herself, "how it can be true that he is living a bad life when he is working so hard."

She remembered how eagerly upon his return he had plunged into the work awaiting him and with what absorption he had devoted himself to it ever since. Repeatedly during the last two or three weeks he had told her that never before had he worked so rapidly and so easily and with such satisfaction in the results.

With keen pleasure and interest she was watching his design for the capitol building take form beneath his fingers, thinking it more beautiful than anything he had done before. Once she had told him, laughingly, that she believed the fairies must come in the night and touch his pencil with magic, else it would not be possible for him to put upon paper so rapidly a thing so lovely.

Only yesterday he had shown her the finished cartoon for the front elevation and with a catch of her breath she had exclaimed, "Oh, Mr. Brand, it is exquisite! I don't know why it is so beautiful, for it looks simple, but, somehow, it seems exactly right."

And he had nodded and smiled in a pleased way and said:

"Yes, that's just it—that's what I wanted to do. It's all in the proportions, and I think, for the first time in my life, I have got them just right."

As she recalled the conversation an automobile whizzed past her, slowed down and returned, and she saw Mrs. Fenlow leaning out and calling to her:

"I thought it was you, Miss Marne! Waiting for a trolley, aren't you? Well, don't wait, jump in with me. I'm going to the city and I'll take you right to your office."

Henrietta had met Mrs. Fenlow a number of times during the long-drawn-out time when the architect was endeavoring to meet her wishes with a design for the country house she had determined to build up the Hudson. She had found the elder woman's open speech and breezy manners amusing, but she had also conceived liking and respect for the sincerity and warm-heartedness that were evident underneath a rather brusque and erratic exterior.

She had been pleased and touched also by the hearty affection and comradeship between Mrs. Fenlow and her only son, Mark Fenlow, her eldest child. Henrietta had met the young man several times in her employer's office and also at his theatre party and house-warming the previous autumn. She knew that Mark had been graduated from college the previous spring and afterwards had been taken into a trust company in which his father was a stock-holder and director and that his mother, who was very proud of him, expected him to climb the ladder rapidly and become an important figure in big financial operations. Henrietta had found him a debonair youth, full of gay humor and high spirits and having, apparently, much of the same kind of good-heartedness and sincerity which she admired in his mother.

"Have you seen the morning paper?" was Mrs. Fenlow's first remark, as Henrietta settled into her seat.

"You mean the accident Mr. Brand had with his automobile? Didn't they have a fortunate escape!"

"That man has the luck of the Irish army!" declared Mrs. Fenlow.

"Did you notice that he was the only one to escape without any injury, though the cause of it was evidently his reckless driving? That's the way things always happen with him. He gets his pleasure and other people take the consequences."

Mrs. Fenlow's tone was so sharp and bitter that Henrietta looked at her in surprise. There were signs of trouble in her face, which bore also something of a war-like aspect. Dark hollows under her eyes and little lines about her mouth seemed to tell of mental anguish. But her lips were pressed together determinedly and she held her head high.

"But he can't go on like this much longer. He's bound to have a smash-up some of these fine days."

"What do you mean, Mrs. Fenlow?" queried Henrietta, wide-eyed.

Mrs. Fenlow had been speaking straight ahead of her, into the air, as if, absorbed in her own bitter thoughts, she had for the moment forgotten her companion. At the girl's question she turned with a quick movement suggestive of the swoop of a bird of prey.

"Pardon me, my dear, if I use disrespectful language about your employer. The Good Lord knows I have reason enough for it. But you needn't feel uneasy because I say it in your hearing, for I'm going to his office this very day to say the same things, and worse, to his face. When I think of the way he's used his influence over Mark—and I believed him the pink of perfection and was as pleased as an old fool over his friendship for my boy! My God!"

Her voice sank to a whisper of such fierce indignation that Henrietta shrunk a little away, staring in astonishment at her set face and quivering lips.

"Of course," she presently went on in a more natural tone, "Mark ought to have known better, he ought to have had more sense and more strength of character than to yield to that sort of temptation. But he was only a lad, and Felix Brand was old enough to know the danger there was in it for a young fellow like that. And Mark admired him so much he thought whatever Brand did must be all right."

She broke off into sudden silence and Henrietta saw her wipe a tear from the corner of her eye. The girl was so confused and embarrassed by these signs of keen emotion and hidden trouble and so ignorant of their cause that she could think of nothing that seemed well to say or do, and so she, too, remained silent until presently the elder woman turned to her again and spoke more gently.

"Don't mind me, my dear. I'm in great trouble—on Mark's account. I've had an awful blow, and I don't know yet how it will all come out. I don't want to be unjust to Felix Brand, but I can't help thinking that he's largely responsible for it. I know he was for the beginning of the whole thing. And I've found out that poor Mark's not the only one—" she was talking off into the air again, oblivious of the girl beside her—"who's paying for the consequences of Felix Brand's private pleasures. It's time he began to pay for some of them himself."

Her voice, quivering with the indignation and anguish she was trying to conceal, subsided into a muttering whose words Henrietta could not distinguish and finally she lapsed into silence. At the door of the building in which was Brand's suite of offices she said to her companion:

"I'm going up with you, my dear, if you'll let me. I want to see Mr. Brand without delay and if he isn't here yet I'll wait for him."

Miss Marne, busy at her desk with the morning's mail, heard sounds from her employer's private room during Mrs. Fenlow's call that betokened a change in the friendly relations formerly existing between them. She could hear the woman's voice raised in what seemed to be bitter denunciation and the man's replying in sneering tones. These seemed so unlike Felix Brand that she paused for a moment in her work, astonished at the unaccustomed note. During the last few weeks she had seen him several times give way to sudden temper, but even these outbursts, unprecedented though they were in her experience of him, had not seemed to her so foreign to his usual affable manner and pleasant speech as did the harsh, sarcastic antagonism of the voice in which she could hear him speaking to Mrs. Fenlow.

"But it must be Mr. Brand," thought his secretary, looking in puzzled wonder at the door into his room, "for there's surely nobody else in there."

As she gazed, held by her surprise, a letter in her hands, the wrathful voices rose again, now one, then the other, and in Mrs. Fenlow's she presently caught the words, "Hugh Gordon."

At that came the sound of the man springing to his feet, of an overturned chair rattling to the floor, of a blow upon his desk and a loud and angry oath. The girl started with a whispered exclamation of amazement and horror. Her shocked ears heard her employer denouncing both Gordon and his caller and heard the rustle of the woman's dress as she hurried across the room.

In her anger and indignation Mrs. Fenlow had rushed to the first door that met her eyes, which chanced to be the one into Henrietta's room. As she opened it she flung back over her shoulder at Brand, in a white heat of scorn and wrath:

"You whited sepulchre! I'm done with you and all my friends shall know what you are!"

She rushed past Henrietta without seeming to see her, and on through the outer room into the corridor. The door into Brand's office was left wide open and Henrietta saw him standing beside his desk, his face so distorted with passion that for a moment she doubted that it was he, and, apparently—and here again she could hardly believe her eyes—shaking his fist at his departing visitor.

CHAPTER XVII

"WHICH SHOULD HAVE THE GIFT OF LIFE?"

There was a chorus of admiration and praise from all over the country when Felix Brand's design for the capitol building was published. It was everywhere recognized as a signal achievement, far in advance of anything he had previously done, and he himself was acclaimed as one of the most promising architects of the time and the most gifted that America had yet produced. Other reproductions of his recent work, business buildings, country houses, a church and a memorial structure, were made public at about the same time and these and the capitol building aroused so much interest that newspapers and magazines published articles about him, with many illustrations of his work and criticisms of his art that praised his present accomplishment in glowing terms and prophesied he would do still greater things. In him, it was declared, had come at last a great American architect, a man of such originality, such skill and such sense of beauty and fitness that, if he continued to give such rich fulfillment of his early promise, he would soon create a distinctly American style of architecture, infused with the national spirit and expressive of the national ideals, worthy to take its place among the great architectures of the world.

His secretary collected these articles and kept them for him to see when he should return. For early in May, just before this round of praise began, when she went one morning to the office she found a letter from him saying that it had suddenly become necessary for him to go abroad at once and that, as he would be sailing in the early morning, he would have to leave affairs once more in her charge. There were some words of praise for her astuteness in the management of his business when he had been away at other times, a few directions concerning things he would like her to do or to leave undone, a brief regret that he should have to leave just now when it was most important for him to be on hand, and the hope that he would not be gone more than three or four weeks at most. But there was neither indication of where, in that large section of the world covered by "abroad," he might be reached by letter or cable, nor mention of which one of the several steamers sailing that day would bear him to his unnamed destination.

Henrietta put the letter down with a sigh of dismay. "It is too bad, too bad!" she exclaimed. "Just when everything is going nicely and he is doing wonderful work! Now things will begin to tangle up again and people will get impatient, and he will lose a lot of money. Well, I'll have to do the best I can until he comes back."

But notwithstanding her devotion to her employer's interests and the deep and genuine pleasure she felt in seeing them advance and in knowing that she was helping to put them forward—the delight of any honest worker in doing well and successfully the thing that he undertakes to do—she soon began to be conscious of a sense of relief at being rid for even a little while of Brand's physical presence. After his violent outburst against Mrs. Fenlow, Henrietta had felt her repugnance increase until it amounted to positive aversion. She did not know how great had been the nervous strain of trying constantly to suppress and ignore this feeling until she was relieved of it by his absence.

"I wonder," she said to herself on her way home a few days later, "if I can endure it long enough after he returns to get entirely rid of that mortgage. Well, I'll have to wait until he does return, anyway, and then I ought to give him, I suppose, two or three weeks' notice. Perhaps, when he comes home this time, he'll be more as he used to be and it won't be so difficult. I'll wait until then before I decide."

As she came to this conclusion she was entering the ticket gate of the ferry waiting room and, lifting her eyes from the dropping of her ticket in the box, she saw a young man of goodly figure, dressed in a loose fitting suit of gray, advancing toward her and lifting his soft felt hat. Even in the surprise of the moment she was conscious of a quick effort to keep out of her countenance the full measure of the joy she felt at this unexpected meeting with Hugh Gordon. But she was not successful enough to hide all signs of the pleasure that swept through her and shone in her smile of welcome.

"Will you let me cross the ferry with you?" he said as he guided her through the crowd to a vantage point near the gate. "I did not go to the office, and I shall not go there again, because I know what orders Felix gave concerning me and I will not subject you to any unpleasant experience with his violent temper."

Henrietta looked at him in surprise, wondering how, since there was evidently bitter enmity between the two men, this one should have such intimate knowledge of the characteristics that had but lately appeared in the other.

"But the ferry boat," he was saying, with one of the smiles that so rarely lighted his serious countenance, "is nobody's private property and you are the only one who can forbid me to ride across the bay in it at just the time when you are going home."

He must have read encouragement rather than objection in her manner, for the next evening he was waiting for her again, and by the end of the week it had become a tacit understanding between them that they should meet thus and take together the ride across the shining evening water. Golden red it glowed and sparkled all about them and spread a radiant path toward the red and gold of the May sunset. Behind them Manhattan reared its mighty, tawny-yellow walls and towers through the golden haze—Mammon rising from the waves, with feet lapped in the rose-gold waters and front ablaze with the diamond dazzle of a thousand sunset-lighted windows.

It was the month of May, nature's month of marvels, when with her magic wand she strikes upon earth, and tree, and plant, and human heart, and the indwelling, everlasting life and youth gush forth in countless streams of leaf and bloom and song and leaping spirit. All through the marvelous month these two rode back and forth every day across the enchanted waters. For it was not long until she began to find him waiting for her in the morning also, at the door of the ferry-house in St. George.

All the world was robed in the young beauty of the spring, but Henrietta Marne soon discovered that for her companion it had but slight appeal. If she, thrilled by the pageant of sunset colors, glowing in the sky and reflected in the waters of the bay, voiced her delight in it Gordon's response would be polite but perfunctory. He would look and make comment, but she knew that it left him cold. If she wore a flower at her belt or her throat, chosen with utmost care to make a tender little harmony of color with her waist or her tie or the faint pink of her cheeks, it nettled her a little that he did not even seem to see it.

"If I do that at the office when Mr. Brand is there," she said to herself, "it's the first thing he sees and he always speaks about it and looks at it with pleasure and he—doesn't care anything about me!"

"I know, it is a defect of my nature," he said one day in response to a little gentle rallying on her part because of his lack of interest in an evening panorama of unusual beauty. "I know I lose a great deal of the pleasure of living because of it, but I can't help it. Something seems to have been left out of my make-up. But I hope that some time I shall recover it. You are so sensitive to these things, perhaps you can teach me how to feel them, too."

Their talk verged soon into the more or less confidential themes of personal viewpoints, experiences and ambitions. Henrietta noticed that Gordon said nothing about his past life, about his relatives or friends or where he had grown up, or gone to school, or what he had done in his youth. But he was full of hopes and plans for the future. His brain was busy working out ideas for large industrial schemes that should prove the possibility of combining reasonable profit for their creators and managers with ample wages, comfortable homes and expanding lives for their workers. In his mind projects were taking form, though vague as yet, for renovating those noisome places of the city where human nature, undiluted by space, stews corrosion and corruption for its souls and bodies. Every day he would give her a glimpse of one or another of a multitude of half formed ideas, perhaps but just conceived, perhaps taking tentative form, which he was eager to work out and put to practical test. For the most part they seemed to her to be an unusual combination of business shrewdness, just feeling, and altruistic intent. Apparently his aim in them was to attain the end of social betterment by means of the co-operative and mutually profitable effort of all concerned in them.

He talked much and with enthusiasm of these things and Henrietta soon found that they and kindred hopes and plans were the purpose and the inspiration of his life.

"I have the business instinct," he told her one day. "It is easy to make money. It is a pleasure, too, to busy one's mind with large schemes and see them coming your way. But that is nothing to the pleasure it will be to set to work, as I shall soon be able to do, upon some of these schemes and see them coming out as I want them to."

"Your pleasure then will be a double one," she said, "the pleasure of creating something and that of doing good as well. Mr. Brand must have that double pleasure, too, when he feels all his faculties at work and knows that he is creating something that is beautiful, as you will feel that you are doing something good."

His face darkened and his eyes flashed at the sound of Brand's name. She felt that he stiffened, mind and body, into hostility.

"Pardon me," he said curtly, "if I am not pleased with the comparison. I consider Felix Brand, his ideas and principles and his mode of life, to be so thoroughly detestable that even the mention of his name rouses my contempt and disgust. I consider him," Gordon went on, his tones lower and more tense, "a plague spot, a source of evil that would be a menace to any community."

"Oh, Mr. Gordon!" she protested. "Aren't you exaggerating dreadfully? Aren't you prejudiced against him? Think of the beautiful buildings he creates and of the elevating and refining influence of such noble and beautiful architecture!"

"I know," he assented, "the man has genius, great genius. He has proved that already, and he might have gone farther in his line and done much finer and greater things, if he had lived a different life. But he is bringing his fate upon himself." He paused for an instant, and she, wondering what he meant by that last dark sentence, which he had spoken in a tone of the most serious significance, was about to ask him for an explanation when he turned upon her abruptly.

"Tell me," he demanded, "do you think that a man is to be pardoned for being a source of evil, for leading or forcing others into wrongdoing and misfortune, while he keeps himself prosperous and honored, just because he can create beautiful things in art, or architecture, or music, or literature? Is the world in greater need of being made more beautiful and more pleasurable for the few than it is of being made better for the many? Would you condone a man for deliberately making it worse because he was adding to its beauty?"

Gordon's intent gaze and the solemn, eager earnestness with which he spoke appalled his listener ever so little. It was as if he were asking these questions from his inmost, deepest heart.

"I—I don't know just what to say," she faltered. "I never thought of the matter in that way before. One doesn't like to answer so serious a question offhand. But—" she hesitated and felt herself being swept into agreement by his very forcefulness of character and intensity of feeling. "Why, yes—I suppose you are right. If the world were entirely wicked it would be a failure, no matter how beautiful it might be."

"I was sure you would agree with me," he responded with a look of pleased satisfaction. "But now I want you to tell me something else," he pursued in a gentler tone and with a humbler, softer manner. "I want to suppose the case of two possible men and I want you to tell me which of the two you think would be the more deserving of life."

He moved closer to her and, leaning against the deck rail, was looking into her face with an expression so different from any she had ever seen in his brown eyes before, wistful and beseeching instead of confident, alert and dauntless, that it set her heart a-flutter with a sudden, tantalizing half-memory. Where, when, had she seen brown eyes with that look in them?

She groped after the answer in the back of her mind while she listened to his voice, still with its impetuous tones unsubdued, though he seemed to be trying to state his hypothetical case in cool, bare terms.

"Suppose there were two men," he was saying, "and suppose that one of them possessed a genius for the creation of noble and beautiful works of art of any sort, which would afford great pleasure to many people and would refine and elevate their tastes. But suppose that at the same time he was living such a private, even secret, life as made him a source of wickedness and corruption, an endless influence for evil. Then would such a man, do you think—" his voice sank lower and thrilled with solemn earnestness—"deserve to live rather than the other one, who, though he had no genius for the creation of beauty, was using all his powers to make the world a better place for all men to live in? If both men could not have the gift of life, Miss Marne, which do you think ought to have it?"

She looked at him, glanced away, and hesitated, her mind still bent on that teasing memory. "You are putting strange riddles to me this morning, Mr. Gordon," she demurred.

Had she ever seen a wild creature expecting destruction at human hands? No, surely not, she told herself, and yet this wistful pleading expression might be just the look in the eyes of an animal facing death but dumbly begging for life.

Then, in a flash, it all came back—her own little parlor, Billikins whining and hiding in her skirts in mysterious terror, and Felix Brand gazing at her with all the usual soft, caressing look of his brown eyes curtained behind some absorbing anxiety and fear. But in these eyes into which she was looking now there was no fear, only a longing that her answer should be what he wished. She shivered as a half-sensed intuition of impending tragedy shot through her.

"You—you make me feel as if I were a judge and called upon to pronounce sentence upon some one," she said and tried to pass the situation off with a little laugh as she added, "Really, it isn't fair!"

But he would not have it so and with even greater earnestness and solemnity pressed his question farther: "Then we'll put it another way. Suppose a mother about to bear a man-child could choose its soul and the life it was to live. Which of those two men would a good, noble woman wish her son to be? Imagine yourself in such a woman's place, Miss Marne, and tell me, which would be your choice."

She felt the compelling force of his earnestness and she was moved by the intense feeling evident in his voice, look and manner. Her face blanched with the sudden conviction that some high consequence hung upon her answer. But she took counsel bravely with herself for a little space as her gaze wandered across the water.

"I think," she replied slowly, "yes, I'm quite sure, any good woman would wish her son to be good rather than great. I don't believe any good woman would hesitate at all, if it were possible for her to make such a choice."

He straightened up and a solemn joy overspread his eyes and face. "I thank you, Miss Marne," he said, barely resting for an instant one hand upon hers that lay on the rail. "I had little doubt what your answer would be, because you are a good woman. But I wanted to know for a certainty. It is my final warrant that I am right."

He said no more, and Henrietta, a little awed by the rapt, triumphant look with which, sitting upright with head thrown back, he gazed into the distance, kept silence also. And in a few moments their ship bumped into its berth and they joined silently the crowd that pressed forward.

After that she was conscious in his manner toward her of an increased air of guardianship. It gave her a warm sense of comfort and security and she found herself gradually confiding in it more and more. She even sought his advice, finally, upon the intimate personal problems that were troubling her so deeply. Did he think she ought to permit her sister to motor with Mr. Brand? Was it likely that she herself could find another situation that would carry her safely out of her financial difficulties if she should continue to find her work under Mr. Brand so disagreeable?

"I hesitate to say anything to you about these things, because I know how much you dislike him," she apologized, "but I feel so uncertain and so much worried about them, and there is nobody else to whom I can go who knows him as well as you do. His whole character has changed so much in the last few months that he hardly seems to be the same man. I have an uneasy feeling that it isn't wise for my sister to go with him, although it does seem the most innocent thing in the world, and the kindest, for him to stop at our house, when he has some business farther down the island, and take Isabella for a spin. She enjoys it so much and she has so few pleasures. And she and mother have such confidence in Mr. Brand that they feel sure he would never ask her to do anything that wasn't perfectly all right. I felt that way, too, at first, but I don't now."

"I am glad you have spoken of it," he replied with interest, "for I have been thinking I ought to give you some warning before Felix returns. He is simply serving a purpose of his own, an utterly selfish purpose, and he is using her to help him gain his end without the least compunction. Don't let her go again, Miss Marne, if you can help it. I know Felix Brand through and through, and he is not to be trusted."

Henrietta could only look at him speechless, her eyes wide with apprehension.

"Don't be alarmed," he hastened to assure her. "I don't think there is anything for you to be uneasy about, except that his influence is always evil—" he paused on a raised inflection and looked at her admiringly. "One of the reasons," he went on regardless of the abrupt change, "why I like you and feel so sure that you are sound and good and strong clear through is because you have not yielded in the least to the subtle influence he has over most people. You have held to your own ideas of what is right and wrong."

She blushed under his eyes and his words. "I'm afraid I don't deserve all that credit. I remember a time when I did have some ugly feelings and some tempestuous desires for pleasures that were out of my reach. But I had too many other things to do and to think about, and so I guess I outgrew them."

"And I guess, too, that they didn't find congenial soil in your heart to take root in," he added. "But you needn't be much worried about your sister, for I am sure it will not last much longer. At the best—or worst—there will not be many more opportunities—" again he straightened up and sent that triumphant glance of his alert, confident eyes out across the water—"in which it will be possible for

136

him to work any evil. But he is so thoroughly base that if I were you I would not trust her with him again."

Henrietta wondered what he meant by that "not many more opportunities," but forebore to ask him lest she might unintentionally pry into some matter of which he did not wish to speak. Another enigmatical fragment from his secret thought came out when she asked his advice about her own relations with Brand. She told him how repugnant she was beginning to find her work because—and here she skipped lightly and diplomatically over her reasons, so that she might not do violence to her own sense of loyalty to her employer—she did not now feel in harmony with his methods of doing business and his ways of looking at a good many things.

"You don't need to put it in so roundabout a way," he told her impulsively. "I know all about that change in the man's character and how nearly he has lost all sense of truth and honesty. Luckily, he still controls his temper with you and treats you with respect——"

He stopped and his whole manner suddenly bristled with aggressiveness. In his voice as he spoke the next words there was a significant ring: "And I don't think he'll do otherwise. But of course you can't put up much longer with these developments in him. I would advise you to look for another position at once. In fact, I am sure you'd better, because it won't be long until Felix will not need you."

She gazed at him with such question and alarm in her eyes, that he returned her look with surprise. "Oh," he exclaimed, "I see. You are puzzled by what I said. I forgot for the moment,—perhaps I have before, too—that you do not know all that I do about Felix. But don't be troubled about it now. Some day you shall know—I shall tell you—the whole story. I dare say it will seem marvelous to you at first. But you will soon see how inevitable it has all been. Felix will return soon, I suppose."

"Oh, I hope so," Henrietta broke in. "He has been gone five weeks and his affairs are in an awful condition!"

Gordon nodded. "Yes, they must be. It is quite time for him to come back and put them in order. But I warn you, Miss Marne, that it will be wise for you not to mention my name to him when he does return. He hates me so furiously and he has so little control over that violent temper he has developed, that there is no telling what he will say or do if any one so much as speaks of me in his presence. You remember his outrageous conduct to Mrs. Fenlow?"

"Oh, did Mrs. Fenlow tell you about that?" Henrietta asked with a quick look of surprise that was reminiscent, too, of the shock the incident had given her. "I thought she mentioned your name. Was that what made him so angry?"

"That was what caused his final brutality. The trouble was about Mark Fenlow. You know how fond and proud of him his mother has been and what high expectations she has always had for him. Felix had got him into the way of gambling and the boy had developed a passion for it which he could not restrain. Ever since Felix has had money he has played a good deal, and for pretty high stakes, because of the pleasure he got out of it. But he knew when to stop, just as he did with all his vicious indulgences."

Gordon's eyes were flashing and his voice growing tense with hostile feeling. But Henrietta saw that he was making a strong effort to keep himself under control and to speak calmly about his enemy.

"That is," he went on, "he used to be able to stop before doing himself injury. He didn't care what happened to others. But he can't now. The gambler's mania has got hold of him in just the same way that he's lost control of his temper, and he's likely, if he keeps on, to gamble away everything he's got. He liked Mark Fenlow and led him into more evil than just the gambling. But it was that that proved the boy's ruin. It was the old story—playing, losing, borrowing, financial difficulties, the temptation of money in sight, the belief that he could pay it back the next day. His last filchings, which brought about discovery and confession of the whole business to his mother and father, were due to the fact that Felix was ruthlessly pressing him to pay back some borrowed money. That was why Mrs. Fenlow went up to Felix's office and told him what she thought of him. Weeks ago I went to the boy and tried to reason with him about the way he was going and persuade him to quit, short off. He told his mother about that, too, and that was how she happened to mention my name in their controversy."

"Poor Mrs. Fenlow!" said Henrietta. "I knew she must be in some great trouble that morning. But what has become of Mark?"

"His father made good his peculations and hushed the matter all up, and then they sent him out west to a cattle ranch."

CHAPTER XVIII

ISABELLA TAKES ONE MORE RIDE

Henrietta Marne looked curiously at the envelope bearing the stamp of Hugh Gordon's business firm. "There is always a letter from Mr. Gordon just before Mr. Brand gets back," she said to herself, "so I suppose he'll be here some time today. If he does I'll have to decide about leaving him. But there'll be such a lot of work to do it won't be fair for me to say anything about going till we get things straightened out again."

On that same June morning Penelope Brand was reading a letter in a similar envelope. She was out of doors, in her wheel-chair, in the shade of that same tree from which she had fallen, years before, to such pitiful maiming of her body and her life. Beside her was a little table holding some books, a pad of paper and a pencil and her work-basket. For here she spent the greater part of every fine day, by turns reading, making notes, writing, sewing, and talking with her mother. The roses that grew along the fence were in bloom and a few steps in the other direction was the little vegetable garden where her mother worked when the sun was not too hot, so near that they could speak to each other now and then.

Penelope was beginning to find a new pleasure in life, the deepest of all pleasures to the woman-heart, the pleasure of service. For Hugh Gordon had been sending her books treating of the sociological questions in which she had long taken an intellectual interest and had asked her to make digests of them for him, to tell him what she thought of them and to write him at length upon such of their contents as seemed to her of particular consequence. She had had a number of letters from him discussing these things and outlining plans upon which he wanted her opinion.

All this was affording her the keenest satisfaction. Her mother, who had never seen her so genuinely happy and contented, beamed with shy delight over the new pleasure that had come into their lives. For her it was sadly darkened by her son's violent antagonism to their new friend. They had learned that they must not mention Hugh Gordon's name to him even in letters, and when he last came to see them, on one of his brief and infrequent visits, they had trembled with anxiety during the whole of his stay lest they might inadvertently approach too near the subject that now loomed so large in the narrow round of their lives and had brought such freshening and broadening of their interests.

They speculated much as to the cause of the animosity between the two men, and it was evident to Mrs. Brand, in all their talk, that her daughter's sympathies were with Hugh Gordon. For Penelope, deep in her heart, well concealed from her mother, had long harbored a feeling toward her brother that was very near distrust and contempt. Mrs. Brand had found in Hugh Gordon and the affection he plainly longed to give and receive, a young man fashioned so much more after her spirit than was her own son that her mother-heart yearned to enfold him also in its love. It grieved her deeply to know how intense was the bitterness between them.

"If they could only both be my boys, and be good friends," she said to Penelope, with brimming eyes.

As Penelope opened her letter from Hugh Gordon she gazed with astonishment at the check it contained, a check for a bigger sum than she and her mother had ever possessed.

"Dear Sister Penelope," she read. "For you didn't say that I mustn't call you sister, and so I shall, because you know that is the way I think of you. I am very happy just now thinking how surprised you will be when you see this check. It is some money that I borrowed of Felix last winter when I wanted to start in business. I am now paying it back to you and your mother instead of to him, because I know that he is not taking care of you as he ought, and also because I know that if I pay it to him he will merely make some bad and wasteful use of it. Enclosed you will find a memorandum of the date, the principal, rate, interest and amount. I shall tell him that I have sent it to you.

"I have wanted very much to see you during this last month, for there are many things to talk over with you at more length than is possible by letter. But I knew what a rage it put Felix into when he learned about my being there the last time and how unhappy his anger and violent talk made both of you, and especially your mother, and I didn't want to subject you to such an experience again.

"But the time is coming soon when I shall be able to visit you as often as you will let me. I am looking forward to that time with such anticipations of happiness as I hardly dare tell you about. If you should decide against me, if you should not feel toward me as I hope you will—but, no, that would not be possible. And so I shall go on thinking of the happy times we shall have when I run over often to see you and when I take both of you upon little trips—to the seashore, to New York, wherever you think you would like to go. For we can make that sort of pleasure possible for you, Penelope, if you want to undertake it.

"It will all be decided and everything explained the next time I see you. But to prepare the way for all that I shall have to tell you, so that you will be ready to listen to it understandingly, I am sending you a book to read in the meantime. You will find in it one of the wonder stories of modern science, and in its light that quick, keen mind of yours will go to the heart of this matter at once. You will see clearly through the essentials of the mystery you have already sensed in the relations between Felix and me. But I hope you will not make up your mind about it until I can explain to you the whole matter, from beginning to end. I think that will be soon, within two or three weeks. In the meantime, you will not hear from me again, for I shall have to go away for a while."

The rest of the letter was taken up with matters about which they had been conferring for some time. But Penelope was not able to find in them her usual interest, so deep was her absorption in Gordon's mystifying allusions and promises.

The anxious wonder they aroused in her, however, was hardly greater than the trepidation and the sense of mystery which descended upon Henrietta Marne as she studied, that same morning, the envelope of Gordon's letter to Felix Brand. Why should such a letter always herald Brand's return from these unaccountable absences, which grew ever longer and of darker omen? What had

Hugh Gordon meant by those two or three curt, unconsidered sentences that seemed to hint at some uncanny fate toward which Brand was hastening? And what would be the architect's demeanor now? Would it be such that she could not stay longer in his employ? With all the financial risk involved would she yet feel that she must go forth and look for another position?

This last question did not long remain unanswered in her mind. Brand's manner, it was true, had not lost entirely its habitual suavity and polish. Formerly she had thought these to be the genuine expression of the innate refinement and kindness of his nature. But now, as if some inner corrosion were eating its way outward, she found that they had ceased to be anything more than the thinnest veneer, through which often broke, in words, or manner, or look, peevish irritation or sullen anger.

"It's as if he were just seething inside," said Henrietta to herself after he had been back several days, "about something or other that makes him too angry to control himself. Well, that's no reason why he should take it out on me, as he did today. I wish I could see Mr. Gordon again. Well, anyway, I can't stand this any longer. I'm sure he'd advise me not to. Mr. Brand is much worse than he was before he went away, and he looks as if he were the bad, base man that Hugh Gordon says he is. I shall tell him at once that he'll have to find another secretary."

When she told her mother and sister that she had decided to look for another position, she had to face a chorus of amazed protests and she found it difficult to convince them of the soundness of her reasons.

"He seems to have lost all sense of honor," she told them. "In all the business that he carries on through me by correspondence and sometimes by my seeing people, too, he lies and cheats even when I can't see, sometimes, that he expects to gain anything by it. And I don't want to be a party to that kind of thing any longer, even if I am only a sort of a machine. And he is growing so ill-tempered and irritable and rude that I really can't endure it."

"Oh, well, don't worry about it, Harry," said Isabella with her usual optimism. "You'll soon get another position. Please make it part of your bargain next time that your employer must come over here and take me out motoring quite frequently, if not oftener."

"That reminds me, Bella, that I want to ask you not to go with Mr. Brand again. I'm sure he's not the kind of man we've always thought him."

"Oh, nonsense!" Bella rejoined, breezily. "Don't be alarmed for your handsome Felix Brand. It doesn't do him a bit of harm and I have a lot of fun. Don't worry about me, Harry. I'm not an infant. And I don't suppose I'll be offered any more perquisites of that sort, now that you're going to leave him. Poor little me!"

Henrietta found her employer in a particularly trying mood the next morning. He looked tired and worn, as though he had not slept, and his mobile countenance, always so eloquent of his state of mind that every changing emotion shone through it as through a window into his soul, told of secret harassment. So also did his tense nerves, which seemed wrought up almost to the snapping point. They vented themselves in frequent bursts of irritability and snarling anger. His secretary noticed that he started at every sudden sound, and sometimes also when she had heard nothing, and that then he would look round him in an alarmed, furtive way, as if he expected to see some menace take form out of the air. To her relief he did not return to the office after luncheon. If she had known that he was speeding in his automobile toward her home she would have taken less comfort in her quiet afternoon.

"Bella, dear, do you think you'd better go?" said her mother. "Harry seems so anxious about it, and she knows him better than we do. Hadn't you better tell you have an engagement, and then take me out for a little walk?"

"Oh, just this one more time won't make any difference, mother! I guess my chatter is good for him, for he always seems blue when we start out, but by the time we come home he's in as good spirits as I am. So it would really be unkind not to go, wouldn't it, mother?"

"Well, dear, if you think best. But I shall be anxious about you, so please ask him to bring you back as soon as he can."

When they returned in the late afternoon Isabella caught a glimpse, as the automobile stopped and she glanced up toward her mother's room, of a man's figure standing beside Mrs. Marne's chair, near the window. Brand helped her out, and then, casting a keen glance at her, with a little laugh he took her by the arm and guided her up the path and across the porch to the door. Fumbling with her key, she scarcely noticed his departure and by the time she stepped inside, his machine was disappearing down the street.

As she entered the hall she saw a man descending the stairs. Looking up uncertainly, she staggered back a little and leaned against the wall.

"Bella!" he cried joyfully, and again, "Bella, darling!" and ran down the steps.

She gave a maudlin giggle. "Warren! Warren! Such s'prise! S' glad t' see you!" she muttered thickly and, lurching toward him, would have fallen had he not caught her.

"Bella! What is the matter?" he exclaimed in anxious tones, and then, in a moment, sudden disgust ringing in his voice: "Bella, you're drunk! My God! And I meant to marry you next month! Motoring with a man and coming home drunk! Good-bye, Miss Marne! It's lucky I discovered my mistake in time!"

He snatched his hat from the rack and slammed the door behind him; and she, as understanding of what had happened dawned upon her, fell forward upon the banister with a long, agonized cry.

Mrs. Marne, lying down to rest in smiling happiness, with her heart full of pleasure as she thought of her dear one's surprise and joy, heard that shriek and hurried in alarm to the head of the stairs. "Bella!" she called. "What is the matter? Where is Warren?"

Isabella, suddenly sobered, lifted a white, drawn face: "Oh, mother, he's gone! He's left me! Oh, mother, mother! It's all over!"

She turned with sudden resolution and fled toward the dining room, so absorbed in her own wild misery that she heard and saw nothing as her mother cried out, swayed to and fro, and then toppled to the floor.

CHAPTER XIX

"AND YOU COULD DO THIS, FELIX BRAND!"

The June afternoon was glowing with sunshine and all the world was clothed in the sumptuous beauty of spring at its highest tide. Henrietta Marne looked about her as she walked slowly up the street toward her home with a heart more at ease than she had known for many weeks. For she had that day secured a position at a salary equal to that she was receiving from Felix Brand and was to begin work in it as soon as the time should expire for which she had already given him notice.

"Difficulties always disappear as soon as you tackle them in real earnest," she was saying to herself as she smiled in pleasure of the green world all about her and of the satisfaction that glowed in her own breast. "Everything is coming out all right. When Hugh Gordon comes back he'll be pleased to find that I've acted on his advice. I'm sorry, awfully sorry, about Mr. Brand—it was so delightful working for him at first, and for a long time—but if he will act like this, what can he expect?"

Glancing upward at the windows of her mother's room as she entered her gate she was surprised not to see there a loving face on the watch for her coming. She opened the front door and the silence of the house struck her heart with a chill of apprehension.

"Mother! Bella!" she called, a flutter of alarm in her tones. "Where are you?"

"Miss Harry! Miss Harry!" came Delia's voice in response. "Do come here, quick, quick!"

She rushed to the dining room and saw her sister stretched upon the lounge and Delia kneeling beside her. On the floor was an empty bottle bearing a death's head and cross-bones and "strychnine" upon its label. She herself had bought it on their physician's prescription, as a tonic for Mrs. Marne, only a few days before.

"What is it, Delia? Did she take that poison?" gasped Henrietta.

"Yes'm, she took it, the whole bottle full. I heard her scream in the hall an' soon she come flyin' in here, an' she snatched up that bottle an' swallowed all them pills before I knew what she was doin'. Then she tumbled down an' I grabbed her an' stuck me finger down her throat. She fought me and tried to push me away, but I wouldn't an' I kep' on stickin' me finger way down an' after a while she spewed it all up. Oh, the dear an' lovely darlin', an' her so merry an' happy all the time! She won't die now, will she, Miss Harry?"

Henrietta had hastily mixed an emetic and together they forced it down her throat.

"I hope she won't, Delia—I hope you've saved her. But we must have a doctor now, at once. Run, Delia, and send the first person you can find as fast as he can go for a doctor to come immediately—say it's a case of life and death."

Delia rushed away and Henrietta, though her heart was full of anxiety about her mother, hovered over Isabella, who lay with closed eyes and ghastly face, moaning but seemingly unconscious.

Presently, fearful of what the silence of the house might mean with regard to its other occupant, she left her sister and hurried upstairs. There she found Mrs. Marne unconscious on the floor. But she knew what should be done and met the crisis with quick and capable action. And in a few moments more she heard in the hall below the voice of their own physician, whom the maid had luckily encountered nearby upon the street.

But scarcely had she supported Mrs. Marne to her bed when a shriek in Delia's voice, followed by the cry of "Doctor! Miss Harry! Come quick!" sent her on flying feet down the stairs again. Isabella, whom she had thought unconscious, had risen and tottered to the kitchen. There the maid, rushing on from the empty dining-room, had found her beside the sink with a bottle of carbolic acid upraised, ready to pour down her throat. Delia had struck it from her hand barely in time to save her from all but a chance burn upon her cheek.

"She must have had some sudden and very serious shock," said the physician later, as he and Henrietta stood beside the bed where Isabella lay, at last sleeping quietly but moaning in her slumber. "Her second attempt to kill herself shows how profound it must have been. But she will come through all right now, I think, though her recovery will perhaps be slow. What she will need more than anything else will be to talk, and as soon as it is prudent you must persuade her to confide in you and tell you the whole story of whatever it was that led her to take this violent measure. Her nature is one that needs sympathy and support, now far more than ever, and the sooner she can be led to pour out all her trouble the sooner she will be able to get her grip on life again. But of course you'll keep all the knowledge of it that you can away from your mother. You'll have to use your own discretion about that. She's had a pretty severe shock, too, and, though she was getting on so well, it's likely to set her back a good deal."

For days Isabella lay in her bed, like a broken, withered flower, weeping much and asking between her sobs why they had not let her die. But at last her sister's love and tender, persistent effort broke through the wrappings of grief and shame that had kept her bound in silence and in Henrietta's arms she sobbed out the pitiful tale that had come to so tragic an ending.

"Oh, Harry," she said, "I can't understand why this awful thing should have happened when I meant no harm at all. I can't see yet that there was anything wrong in my going out with Mr. Brand now and then. It wasn't many times, you know, and always he had some business errand and just stopped for me to give me a little pleasure and to have some company himself. I suppose he liked to have me go with him because I was always jolly and kept him in good spirits. For I did notice, Harry, that when he came he always seemed rather blue and anxious, and then, after we had been out for a while and I had laughed and chattered a lot, he would be more cheerful and by the time we would get back he would seem quite himself again.

"Since I have been lying here and thinking and thinking, Harry, dear," she stopped and hid her face and a shiver of shame passed over her body. Henrietta's arms tightened about her and she whispered soothing, loving words. "I've been thinking, dear," Isabella went on brokenly, "that perhaps that was why he always stopped somewhere and ordered a bottle of champagne. Because it did put me in such gay spirits and, I suppose, made me more lively and just that much better company. And that, I guess, was what he wanted. I never drank but little, never more than a glass or two, and I couldn't see any harm in it, though you did think I oughtn't. Sometimes I held back and asked him if he thought I'd better, and he always laughed at me and urged me on and made it seem silly in me to have scruples.

"But that last day—" again she stopped and broke into a passion of sobbing that took all of Henrietta's loving sympathy and tenderness to soothe. "You asked me not to go again," she went on after a while in trembling tones, "and when he came mother, too, thought I'd better not. Oh, Harry, how I wish I had heeded you and refused to go! I could have made some excuse, and then—Oh, Harry, Harry, I don't want to live any longer!"

"There, there, darling!" soothed her sister. "Try to control yourself and tell me all that happened. I'm sure it couldn't have been anything so very bad. Tell me all about it, dear, and then you'll feel better."

"Mr. Brand seemed so different from what he used to be," she presently went on, "and I began to understand what you told us about the change in him. I was just a little afraid after we started, he seemed to be in such an ugly temper and, oh, Harry, what a bad man he looks now! I begged him to bring me home again after a little while, but he wouldn't and said his business was too important to be put aside for my whims.

"I was a little frightened and a good deal anxious and so of course I wasn't as gay as usual, and that seemed to make him angry. Then he said we'd stop and have some wine and I thought perhaps it would be best to humor him and then maybe I could persuade him to bring me home. I meant not to drink more than a glass, but he made me— perhaps he thought it would make me more lively. Anyway, he was so rough in his manner and looks and there was such an angry gleam in his eyes that I was too frightened not to do what he told me to. And by the time we got home I was—oh, Harry, I can't say it—and Warren met me as I came in and saw—and he said—an awful thing—and rushed away—and it's all over, Harry—I can never see him again—it's all over."

"Don't think that, yet, Bella, dear. I'll write to him and explain it all, and he'll know it wasn't your fault. He won't blame you. He's too kind-hearted and good not to see that it was hasty of him to act as he did."

"That won't matter, Harry. I'd like him to know that I'm not the kind of woman he seemed to think. But I could never, never look him in the face again after—that—after what he saw and said. I'd always think he was thinking of it. It's all over, Harry, it's all over."

When at last Henrietta had soothed her sister to sleep she stood beside the bed looking down at Isabella's grief-stricken face and listening to the sobs that now and then convulsed her throat.

"And you could do this, Felix Brand!" she said bitterly. "You, that we thought so noble and good! Hugh Gordon is right—you are a wicked man, and if you are the one he meant you don't deserve to live!"

CHAPTER XX

"SAVE ME, DR. ANNISTER!"

Mildred Annister, passing the open door of her father's waiting room, sent into it a casual glance, came to a sudden stop, and then, with a brightening face, went quickly in, saying softly, "Felix!" Sweeping the room with her eyes she saw that he was its only occupant and ran toward him, holding out her hands and asking, apprehensively:

"Felix! You're waiting to see father! Are you ill?"

She put her hands upon his shoulders and studied his face with anxious scrutiny for an instant, until, yielding to the pressure of his arms, she sank upon his breast with a murmur of happy laughter.

"No, dearest, I'm not ill—you can see how perfectly well I look. It's just a little nerve tire, I guess, and I want to ask Dr. Annister to prescribe a tonic for me. It's nothing of any consequence."

She drew back and studied his face again. Even her fascinated eyes began to see in it something different from the look of the man who had won her love so completely a year before. She was conscious of a little shiver, that meant, she knew not what, but kept her from yielding when he would press her again into his arms.

"I'm afraid—Felix, dear—I know you must be working too hard. That's what's the matter and that's what makes you look—a little—strange. You are tired. You are doing such lots of work. And you mustn't break down—now!" With another happy, loving little laugh she gave up and nestled against his shoulder, while he kissed her cheek and brow and lips.

"Felix!" she exclaimed, "I'm standing out bravely against that trip to Europe father is so determined I shall take with mother this summer. I won't go and leave you. He hasn't said so much about it lately, because he's not well and mother is anxious about him. I've almost persuaded her that she ought not to leave him."

She paused a moment, her face rosy with his caresses. Her eyes sought his and her voice sank to a whisper. "Felix, dear heart, if we could only go there alone together! Can't we tell them and then just go away by ourselves?"

"I don't think we'd better tell them yet. Your father seems to have become opposed to us, for some reason, and I'm trying to win him over. We must wait a little."

"It's only because he can't bear to think of my marrying any one. He doesn't want to give me up——"

"I don't blame him for that!"

"But he'll have to some time, and—oh, Felix! I wish we could tell him, and mother, soon! It makes me feel so underhanded, and it mars my happiness, just a little, darling. Don't you think it would be better to face the music and have it over with?"

The sound of Dr. Annister's voice dismissing a patient came to their ears and she sprang out of his embrace. "No, no! don't whisper a word of it," he hastily adjured her. "We must wait a little while longer. Remember what I say." There was a touch of impatience, almost of roughness, in his tone as he spoke the last words that made her turn wondering eyes upon him for an instant. But her father was opening the door into his consulting room and now came forward with an outstretched hand. She put her arm through her lover's and walked with him into the office.

"This naughty boy has been working too hard, father," she said gaily, "and he has that tired feeling. I think you'd better prescribe a six months' rest and a trip around the world!"

She was smiling persuasively at her father and did not see the look of irritation that leaped into Brand's eyes as he turned them suddenly upon her. Then he laughingly shook his head, saying:

"It would be a bigger dose than I could swallow, I'm afraid. I have too many contracts on my hands now to be able to take any such French leave as that."

153

"Anyway, father," she insisted as she moved toward the door and, from behind the doctor's back, threw her lover a kiss, "you must tell him not to overwork himself, as he's been doing lately."

"Well, Felix, what is it? What's the trouble?" said the little physician kindly, as he sank back into the depths of his capacious arm-chair.

But the architect was ill at ease. He sprang up from the chair where he had just seated himself and began walking back and forth in the narrow space. His whole soul was in rebellion against the confession he had come there to make.

"Perhaps you will remember, Dr. Annister," he began, broke off, stopped to wipe his brow, then stumbled on: "It was here in your office—you will remember, when I recall it to you—some time ago, you told me—you asked me about—certain things, and urged me to come to you—if at any time I felt I needed your help."

"Yes, yes, I remember," the doctor rejoined in encouraging tones. He was looking at Brand with a searching gaze and saying to himself: "Faugh! How repulsive his face has grown! He's going to tell me the whole truth this time!"

Brand was silent again and the doctor went on, a little more briskly: "Well, let's begin and have it over with. You must bear in mind that the secrets of the physician's office are as sacred as those of the confessional."

"I know it, Dr. Annister. But it's a strange story I have to tell you, and I don't know whether or not you can help me. I thought I could fight it out myself and win, but I can't. And if you can't help me God knows what will become of me."

His voice sank despairingly and he dropped into the chair again, his face in his hands.

"I'll do my best, Felix, whatever it is," the other encouraged again. "Don't hesitate to confide in me. I've listened to many, many strange stories in this room, and only the walls are any the wiser."

"I suppose I'm ill." Brand started up again and moved about with uneasy steps. "I believe you physicians have decided it's an illness—and I think you've treated some cases—" he halted and seemed to gather up resolution for his next words—"dissociated, or dual, personality—that's what you call it, isn't it?"

Dr. Annister sat bolt upright and for an instant could not put under professional control the surprise that crossed his face. But Brand, half turned away, was gazing at the floor as if he found it difficult to meet his companion's eyes. He was conscious of an edge of impersonal interest in the physician's voice:

"Yes, I've done a little in that line—a few cases—but nothing to equal in importance the work of one or two others. But I've been pretty successful. Doubtless I can help you. Go on. Tell me about it."

"It's that damned Hugh Gordon!" the architect broke out, turning savagely toward the doctor, his face distorted with anger and his eyes blazing. "He's fighting me for my body! He said he'd push me off the edge, and he's doing it. Save me, Dr. Annister! Save me from him! Send him back to where he came from!" In sudden realization of the fate that threatened him Brand sank trembling into his chair.

"I'll try, Felix, I'll do my best, and I'm sure I can help you. But you must tell me everything about it. How long has this condition been going on? When did it begin?"

"Oh, I hardly know how to answer that, it came about so gradually. Last fall, in October, was the first time he—he—came out. But long before that he was alive, inside of me, and I knew about him sometimes in my dreams. For years, ever since I was a boy, I have had occasionally a curious experience in a dream. I would be in the dream always, but not as myself. I would know, in the dream and afterwards, that it was I who was feeling, thinking, acting, talking, but at the same time it would seem to be an entirely different personality. Of course there is always more or less of that feeling in a dream, but in this case the divergence was so sharp and the consciousness of a different individuality was so distinct that it was just as if my mind, or soul, or whatever it is that holds the essence of myself, had left me and taken possession of some other individual.

Can you tell me what that meant, Dr. Annister? For it was the beginning of the whole business, and I've thought, sometimes, that I might have saved myself all—*this*. Do you think I could?"

Dr. Annister was gazing at his patient with inscrutable eyes, sitting upright, his fingers tapping. "I can't say now, Felix. I don't know enough yet. But this experience was probably due to your subconscious self. For we are pretty well assured that there is an existence, perhaps more than one, in every human being subordinate to that of which he is conscious, which is himself. Submerged beneath the full stream of his conscious existence, with all its phases of physical and psychical activity, this other existence goes on. In most people it is either so deeply submerged or so closely bound up in their conscious existence that they never know anything about it. Sometimes they catch dim glimpses of it, and once in awhile, in one person out of many millions, some nervous shock will break the bonds between the two and the submerged consciousness will rise to the surface and take possession. That is probably what happened in your dreams, with, doubtless, some shock at the beginning to make it possible. Did these dreams occur frequently?"

"I don't think they did at first. But I was too young and thoughtless to take any account of them. I remember that they occurred once in a while in my teens. Afterwards they became more frequent and the impression they made upon me was much stronger. Then that impression began to remain with me after I was awake, more as a memory at first, an unusually vivid remembrance of a dream state. Then it grew so strong that for an hour or two after waking it would dominate me and I could feel myself almost swaying back into that other person I had been while I was asleep and dreaming. I thought it would be a curious and interesting experience if I could slip over into this other person sometimes while I was awake. You know you get rather tired sometimes of your own individuality."

He stopped and smiled, then went on: "It has never been my habit to pass by any interesting or pleasurable experience that came my way."

The smile became almost a leer and then stiffened into a sneering defiance as his gaze met the clear gray eyes of the physician, impersonal, professional, unresponding. The doctor's chin rested upon his locked fingers and his eyes were fastened upon the other's face. Brand did not know how much of his soul that searching gaze was gradually forcing him to reveal.

"I have always thought," he went on, as if moved by an impulse of self-defense, the half-leering, half-sneering smile still on his face, "that a man has the right to sample all the pleasures that come within his reach. It's the only way by which he can come into full knowledge of himself, and so reach his highest development. And that, I take it, is one of the things a man lives for. Therefore he owes it to himself to let nothing pass by him untried."

Brand ceased speaking and waited as if he expected some response. "Don't you agree with me?" he said, after a moment of silence, in his old, suave and deferent manner.

"Eh? Agree with you? Oh, my opinion on that matter is of no consequence just now. You were speaking about this other individuality beginning to dominate you after you awoke. What happened then?"

The architect straightened up and sent an irritated glance toward his companion. But that clear gaze had established too firm a hold over his will to be swayed by sudden temper. He fidgeted in his chair, then took up his story again:

"Yes, I wondered what it would be like really to be somebody else now and then. The dream was no more real to me than any dream ever is, and if I could let myself be this other individuality for a little while awake it seemed to me that it would be a wonderful experience—something that nobody else had ever had. One morning last fall I woke up with the remembrance of such a dream particularly vivid and the impression of this other personality stronger than it had ever been. It seemed to me that if I so much as shut my eyes I'd drift off into this other being. While I was dressing I thought I'd just try it and see what would happen. I was getting ready to shave and as I made up my mind, or, rather, took down my determination against it, I happened to look at the bright blade of my razor. It seemed as if my eyes fairly stuck fast to it for a moment and—the thing was done."

The doctor nodded. "Yes. Self-hypnosis. Go on. The case is most interesting."

"Well, for about an hour I was—the Lord knows where or what. When I came to myself again I had no recollection of what had taken place. Except for the clock I wouldn't have known that any time at all had passed. I found that I had shaved myself, and had left my mustache, but what else I had done I don't know. I tried it again a little later, hoping I might, if I knew what was coming, be aware of what happened. But I wasn't. I completely lost my own consciousness for that time.

"Then this—this creature was able, after that, to come out of his own will, without my giving permission. He would come while I was asleep, at first only for a few hours, and he would usually leave a letter for me in the room telling me what he had done and what he wanted me to do. He called himself 'Hugh Gordon' and always signed his letters that way.

"At first I thought this was rather amusing. But each time that he came his power grew stronger, and so did his desire for an independent existence. Before long he was taking possession of my body for a day or two at a time, going out and following his own affairs. He bought a suit of gray clothes—he seemed to want everything different from me—and when at last he was able to keep himself going for a week or two he had my hair cut short and let a mustache grow, and began sending his damned insolent letters through the mail to my office.

"Now you know, Dr. Annister, why I couldn't explain my absences any better. Each time that he pushes me down and gets possession of my body he keeps it longer. Now he's threatening me with annihilation. He says that the next time he comes he's going to stay. And I'm at the end of my strength, doctor. I've fought him back, and he's fought to get out, for hours, and days. It's worst at night, because, so far, the change has always taken place when I was asleep. For the last two nights I have not slept—I've been afraid to close my eyes. I've tramped up and down my apartment and I've drank brandy and I've gone around town and raised hell. But I can't fight him off much longer and I've got to have some sleep. Unless you can help me I've come to the end."

Dr. Annister was looking at him gravely, sympathetically, the deepest interest manifest in his countenance. "I hope I can help you, Felix. I hope I can. We'll try. I wish you had come to me with this long ago. It might have been easier. But I need to know still more about it. The case is very peculiar, very interesting, and it has features that differentiate it from any other that has been studied by any physician. These dreams that the whole thing seems to have grown out of—try to remember, Felix, were they preceded by any severe nervous shock, an illness, anything that might have aided in the breaking up of your personality?"

Brand hesitated and a faint color crept into his face. He knew when they began and it was a thing he did not like to think of, even now, after so many years and the change which these later months had made in his character. But the doctor's gaze was upon him and he felt compulsion in it.

"I think," he said slowly, "it must have been perhaps twenty years or more ago. I had just entered my teens. My sister and I were in a tree in our yard and she fell out and was badly hurt. She—she has never recovered. It was a good deal of a shock to me. I began to notice the dreams soon afterward. But they weren't very frequent."

"Just so. It might have been that." The doctor was tapping his finger-tips together thoughtfully. There was something he wanted to know, which he must find out. But he did not believe that the man before him would answer truthfully the questions he needed to ask. So he decided to experiment in another direction. "This—this other you," he went on, "this Hugh Gordon, came to see me once and——"

"Don't call him my other self!" Felix cried out angrily, jumping to his feet and scowling. "He is a thief, a murderer! He has stolen my good name, my money, my body, he is trying to kill me! I know he came here and tried to poison your feeling against me—and I think he must have succeeded, too. He has tried to set my own mother and sister against me in that same way. He goes snooping out to their home and makes them believe all sorts of tales about me. He's even been whispering his lies into the ear of my secretary, until she's going to leave me."

In his rage, which grew with each fresh accusation that he brought against his enemy, Brand was rushing about with uneven steps and now and then smiting a table or a chair with his fist. "He is determined to pull me down and cover me with disgrace and then annihilate me for his own benefit. Damn him, I won't have him spoken of as my other self!"

"Try to be calm, Felix," urged the doctor quietly. "You only make your task the harder every time you give up to such outbursts of rage." He was looking at the other's trembling hands and working face and thinking that here was at least a beginning of what he wished to know.

"Has this abnormal condition affected you in the exercise of your special gift?" he asked. Brand's face brightened and his manner quieted at once.

"Ah! That's something he's not been able to filch from me, the damned thief!" he exclaimed exultantly as he seated himself again. "I've kept all the talent I ever had in that line, and it has developed and increased wonderfully—I don't mean to boast, Dr. Annister, but I know what I'm talking about—since this has been going on. If you saw the pictures that were published and the things all the critics said of me a few weeks ago you would know that is true. I'm astonished myself lately at the ease, the rapidity and the success with which I work. But it's all he has not stolen," Brand continued more gloomily. "He has taken all my business sense. I used to have a good deal of it. I could make money and I would soon have been a rich man. Now I'm getting poorer every day, and he's getting rich."

"Yes, I see." The physician was nodding and softly beating his fingers together. "I get an idea of how the cleavage has been. Your nature was broken into two parts—as clean and sharp and complete a break as in any case I know of. Our task now is to reunite them and make a whole man again out of the halves into which you have separated."

Brand leaned forward eagerly. "Then you'll help me?" he demanded. "You won't go over to his side? The damned hypocrite! He says he is more entitled to life than I am, because he's a better man, because he wants to do good. Why, Doctor, in the last letter he sent me—" Brand's anger was rising again—"he ordered me to make my will, and to leave a letter for some one that would explain my disappearance so that it would be known that I was gone for good, that I was never coming back!" The physician held his patient with a calm gaze and made a sign that he was to control himself. And in a moment Felix sank back into his seat, trembling with the reaction from his burst of temper, and imploring the other for the gift of a longer lease of life.

"You'll send him back to where he came from, won't you, Dr. Annister? You won't let him have his will over me?"

"We can succeed," the doctor assured him in confident tones, "if you will do your part. You must control yourself at all times. Try to strengthen your enfeebled will power. Live quietly, sanely, and a clean, moral life. I don't believe you've been doing that, Felix."

"Oh, I've had to keep some excitement going. I've motored like the devil all around New York, and when I could have pleasant company with me that helped to hold that damned creature down as much as anything. Some people were better than others. Miss Marne's sister, a jolly girl, especially if I fed her with champagne while we were out, was very useful and she saved me several times. But the last time it was a failure. She seemed to be afraid of me and though I made her drink wine till she was drunk, it was no good. I came back no better off than I was before."

Dr. Annister made a sudden movement and looked at his watch. He was conscious of an irruption of unprofessional loathing into his feeling for his patient. He was wondering how much this callous disregard of everything but his own interest was due to his abnormal condition and how much to his innate selfishness; and his thoughts flew to his own cherished daughter.

"Well, Felix," he said rising, "I'm due—I've barely time to make it—at a consultation over an important case, so that we can't go any farther into this now. But I can help you. I'm sure I can, if you will follow orders. I shall try hypnosis. It's the only thing we know, yet, that really has much effect. But some wonderful cures have been made with it. Come back tonight. My evening office hour is from eight to nine. Come about nine o'clock, so that I can take you the last one and have plenty of time for experiment. And there's another thing, Felix,—ah!" He stopped suddenly, as a little spasm of pain crossed his face, and pressed his hand against his heart. "It's nothing," he went on deprecatingly, at the other's look of inquiry. "This little organ in here," and he patted his breast, "reminds me of its existence, once in a while, lately. I'm ordered to take a rest, and I suppose I'll have to before long."

"You're not going away?" Brand queried anxiously. "You won't go till after you've fixed me up?"

"I can't go for some time—unless I have to. And don't mention it to Mildred or Mrs. Annister. Now, about that other thing. I must insist, Felix, that you release Mildred from this engagement between you. I have let it go on against my own judgment too long already, because I was hoping that time would lessen her infatuation. But in the light of all that you have just told me it is impossible—it must not continue another day. You ought to see yourself how unfair it would be to her."

"But suppose," said Brand, with the suggestion of a sneer in his voice, "that Mildred should not wish to be released?"

The doctor pressed his lips together and his gray eyes flashed. His pale face looked very weary. "Her wishes can make no difference now," he replied decisively. "Write to her and say that you wish to end the engagement. Make any excuse that you like. But you must not see her again. That is final, Felix. Good-bye. I'll see you tonight."

CHAPTER XXI

HUGH GORDON TELLS HIS STORY

Dr. Annister dismissed his last patient and looked at his watch. It was nine o'clock and Felix Brand, he thought, was probably in the waiting room. His face was even paler than usual and its deep lines told of pain, anxiety and spent strength. He sat down, his head upon his hand and his thoughts upon his daughter.

"Poor child!" he said to himself. "It will go hard with her. But there can be no 'ifs' or 'ands' about it now. Her mother must take her away where there will be no possibility of her seeing him again. Poor little girl!"

He rose with a weary sigh and crossed to the door into the waiting room. As he threw it open a man at the farther side of the room arose and came toward him with a quick, firm stride and a confident manner. He saw at once that it was not Felix Brand.

"Good evening, Dr. Annister," said the stranger. "I know you were expecting to see Mr. Brand, but I have come in his place. I am Hugh Gordon."

"I am glad to see you, Mr. Gordon," the doctor replied, his interest at once at high pitch. "You can tell me the other side of the case. I met you once before, I believe. Will you come in?"

The physician cast a keen glance at his visitor and said to himself, astonished, that he would never have believed this physical envelope to be the same that housed the man with whom he had talked a few hours before. Feature and coloring were there, it was true, but a different soul animated the body and lighted the countenance and made of the whole another man. The tell-tale signs of evil living had vanished from the face, and so also had its expression of ultra refinement and sensitiveness, while in the eyes no longer shone that winning, caressing look which had been a magnet for the hearts of women. This man held his head high, his eyes were keen, penetrating, virile, and in his countenance the doctor read sincerity, forcefulness, determination. "'As he thinketh in his heart, so is he'," Dr. Annister mused as he leaned forward to listen to what the young man was saying.

"I have come to tell you the truth about this matter, so that you can see for yourself that Felix Brand is not worth saving. You promised him this morning that you would help him. But when you hear what I can tell you I have no doubt you will feel, as I do, that he deserves the fate he has brought upon himself and that the world will be better to be rid of him."

"One moment," said the doctor. "Were you aware of all that passed between us this morning? Do you know all that happens to him?"

"Everything he thinks and says and does I know, and I have always known. That is one of the reasons why I have determined that he must go. I will no longer be a witness within his body of his evil deeds. I am never unconscious, as he is always when he goes under. And that is why, also, I am able to tell you the simple truth. It is not so strange a story as you may think. I wonder sometimes why something of the sort has not happened to many a man.

"It began with that incident about his sister of which he told you. But it wasn't an accident. He wanted her seat on the limb of the tree and when she wouldn't give it to him he pushed her off. She was almost killed and was crippled for life. But nobody, except him and her and me, has ever known that it was not an accident. He surrendered to selfishness and cowardice and for the first time in his life denied his conscience. That was the beginning of me, and of all that has happened since."

Dr. Annister was leaning forward, almost out of his chair, and so intense was the interest with which he was listening that his pale face was alight and its lines of anxiety and fatigue smoothed out.

"I see!" he exclaimed eagerly. "I begin to understand how it was. The shock, the struggle within himself and the revulsion of his conscience from the victory won by the worse side of his nature started up a new center, or threw off a new nebula, of consciousness—we can only vaguely guess at the process. It proved

164

strong enough to form within his brain the embryo of another individuality.

"I have thought sometimes—" the doctor stopped for a moment, his attention turning inwards again, while his elbows sought the arms of the chair and his finger-tips came together. "I am beginning to believe," he went on, his gaze fixed high up on the wall, "that even in apparently normal human beings there may exist two or more of these nebulæ of consciousness in process of formation, but bound up so closely with the dominating consciousness that they never quite separate themselves. The case never becomes that of complete dual personality, although such a person may have within himself two widely different sets of ideals and principles of living.

"Strangely enough, these cases seem always to be evolved out of the person's attitude toward the ethical problems of life. There, for instance, are the officers of powerful corporations who may be rapacious, ruthless, brutal, criminal, in their business methods, but in private life the kindest, most sympathetic and generous of men. Yes, I am beginning to think it may be that such men have set going within themselves some such physiological and psychological process as this which has nearly overwhelmed Felix Brand.

"Who can tell what a few more years of investigation and study of this problem will give us!" The finger-tips were rhythmically tapping and the physician's face was alight with interest, although he seemed for the moment to have forgotten his companion. "Perhaps in another generation or two we shall have discovered that it is medical not legal treatment that pirate captains of industry stand in need of. Perhaps the too shrewd financiers of that day will not be fined or sent to prison but compelled to take courses of hypnotic treatment."

Dr. Annister's gaze, wandering downward, fell upon his companion, and he came back to the matter in hand with a deprecatory smile.

"Pardon me, Mr. Gordon. I've been going far astray. But the whole question interests me deeply. Strange, strange, what havoc within a man's brain that war between right and wrong can make, when his own fierce desires get mixed up in it! Will you go on, please? After this first act of cruelty, unintentional doubtless, but afterward concealed, out of cowardice and the desire to advance his own selfish interests—then?"

"Why, it was the beginning of a constantly growing habit of selfishness in thought and action. I could tell you of thousands of little incidents, each of which helped to strengthen his conception of himself as the center of everything and his notion that his wishes must be gratified and his desires satisfied, at whatever cost to others. This didn't come all at once, you know. It was the growth of years, and kept on all through his youth and early manhood, till it reached its present abominable state. And as it grew, so did I."

"Yes, yes!" the physician broke in again. "Every impulse toward altruistic thought or action that was denied broke off and attached itself to the other nebula of consciousness. Thus he set up within himself two centers of consciousness, of moral growth, one altruistic and the other egotistic. And, as these grew, certain other mental qualities were caught within them, so that, when the separation was at last complete, each individuality had, intensified, the qualities that, mingled together, ought to have gone to the making of an evenly balanced, highly endowed man."

"That's it. And now the question is, which of us are you going to try to save? Which will you allow to live?"

"Why, I'm going to try to put you together again, to mingle you into one proportioned, rounded individuality."

Gordon's manner bristled with aggressiveness. "You can't do it," he exclaimed abruptly. "It's beyond human power, now. 'All the king's horses and all the king's men' wouldn't be enough for such a job. Felix Brand is beyond saving. He chose his part and wilfully kept in it. Let him suffer the consequences. I was his conscience—the part of him in which conscience abode. He denied me and repulsed me over and over again, until he so calloused himself that there was no point left for attack. And so we have become two separate and complete human beings."

Gordon's words were rushing forth in an impulsive torrent and the physician held up an arresting finger. "No, you're wrong there. You are not two complete human beings. It has come about that he has divested himself of moral sense. But he still has a wonderful esthetic gift, of very great value to the world. Have you any part in that?"

"No, I have not," was Gordon's quick reply. "I admit I am lacking on that side of my nature. But is that the most important thing for a man to possess?"

He sprang to his feet and strode about as he went on pouring out his arguments with emphatic, forceful manner. Dr. Annister watched him, wondering at his apparent size. For he looked a considerably larger man than did Felix Brand. The light gray clothing, of looser fit, made some difference, but the physician decided that his manner was responsible for most of the illusion—his self-confident stride, his masterful quality, the impression he gave of abundant vitality and of strength of character and of body. These were all in strong contrast to Brand's courtly, winning manners, affable tones and leisurely, graceful movements.

"Felix Brand has become a monster, a swollen toad of egotism. He cares for nothing but his own advantage, his own interests, his own pleasures, and these he reaches out and takes, grabs them, without any regard for other people's rights or necessities. That kind of selfishness is the root of all evil, and Felix Brand is its incarnation. He is soaked with wickedness. Oh, you do not know the half of it, Dr. Annister, though you have guessed something from the change in the expression of his countenance. For years he has been like a carrier of typhoid, spreading the contagion of his own sinful nature wherever he went, himself unpunished, even admired, looked up to and patterned after. Do you want to keep such a man alive? Do you think, do you really believe, Dr. Annister, that the genius of such a man as that, whatever it is, could make amends to the world for all the evil that he does?"

"You forget, Mr. Gordon, that it is no part of my purpose to keep him as he is. It is my duty to save him from the consequences of his folly and of his perverted view of his relations with the world—to make him whole again."

"You can't do it, Dr. Annister, you can't do it! Oil and water will no more mix than my characteristics and his can be made to mingle in a smooth blend again. My purpose in life is to add to the well-being of the world. I want to lessen its poverty and its degradation and help to reform the soul-poisoning conditions under which so many thousands live. I have planned my life and my head is full of schemes for the betterment of the world. I find it easy to make money. I shall be rich soon. My chief interest and pleasure will be in using my money to work out those plans. It is not my intention to do this as charity or according to ordinary, philanthropic methods. I've no use for charity. It is wrong and it only makes things worse. What I purpose doing is to carry out my business schemes by such methods as will enable those who work with me and for me to earn their own betterments in life, and then to enlighten and guide them in the spending and investment of their earnings. I want to prove that that sort of thing is possible and profitable. In that and similar ways, which will benefit and make others happy quite as much as they will contribute to my satisfaction, I expect to spend my life. Felix Brand will design some beautiful buildings. But he will add to the rottenness of the world and spread disaster and misery with every day of his life. Will the buildings atone for all that evil?"

Dr. Annister's person, sunk in the depths of his arm-chair, looked even smaller than usual, in comparison with this energetic, dominating figure that stood above him, speaking with emphasis and conviction, instinct with determined will. He leaned forward and began to tap his finger-tips, his face thoughtful. Silence fell upon them for a moment.

"My mission," he presently said, slowly and solemnly, "is to heal, not to judge. But," he added, in a mournful tone, "you give me an idea of what a splendid man Felix Brand might have been if he had not so perverted and maimed himself."

Gordon made a gesture of impatience and his dark eyes flashed. "He chose his way. Let him walk in it. I did my best to warn him where it would lead. As long as I lived in him, I was his conscience and tried to plead with him and argue with him. After I broke from him and began to live my own life I wrote letters to him and told him the sort of creature he was becoming and what he might expect.

"It was as if we were twins, with only one body between us. At first I felt strongly the bond that held us together. At the start I did not want to do anything to injure him. I thought we might both live, taking turns with our one body. But as soon as I tried to make him see the evil of his ways he began to hate me. His life grew so much worse that I lost all patience with him. He would pay no attention to my warnings.

"When he decided that he wanted that appointment to the Municipal Art Commission, of course, characteristically, he wanted it at once, by fair means or foul. I warned him not to do anything underhanded and he told me to mind my own affairs. I told him I'd show him up if he dabbled in any unscrupulous methods. But he went straight ahead after what he wanted. You know what the consequences were."

"Yes, I remember," the physician assented. "It was almost my first intimation, really my first proof, that Felix was not what I, and everyone, had thought him."

"Oh, he had kept the outside of his life as admirable as any one could wish. But I knew, long before that, how dirty and misshapen his soul was. Even then, though, if he had heeded my warnings and shown any desire to straighten out his theory of life and clean up his methods of living I would have done my best to help him. At that time I would even have given up my own desire to live and tried to reincorporate myself with him. But it was no good, any of it.

"There was the case of that young woman, Miss Andrews, a nice girl, with talent, and likely to make a fine success in her profession. But Felix Brand crossed her path, took a fancy to her, talked his damnable ideas into her head and set her feet on the downward path. She's going down now at a lively rate, thanks to the lessons she had from him, and she'll soon be at the bottom. It was that incident as much as any one thing that determined me I'd live my own life, and the whole of it, and let him work out his own damnation as fast as he could. I didn't want to be instrumental in continuing his life as such a source of evil. Do you, Dr. Annister?"

The little physician sat with his finger-tips softly beating together, his attention all in drawn and his thought concentrated upon the problem which had been proposed to him. At last he rose slowly to his feet and turned his gray eyes upon Gordon, whose intent gaze was fastened upon his face.

"Your meaning, as I understand it, Mr. Gordon, is that I should refrain from giving him any assistance. And you believe that you can, in that case, dominate him completely, force him out of consciousness, keep him out of it, and yourself enjoy, from that time on, uninterrupted, active life, in his body."

"That is what I think I shall be justified in doing."

"Then I must tell you that I cannot help you. My Hippocratic oath binds me to the healing, the saving of life. He is my patient. He came to me asking my aid. I must give it to him, to the best of my ability."

Hugh Gordon straightened up and threw back his head. It seemed to his companion almost as if his body grew suddenly larger in the tensing of his purpose and his will.

"And I must tell you, Dr. Annister," he exclaimed, his eyes flashing and his face determined, "that I shall succeed in spite of you both. You cannot make a good man out of him; and it is outrageous, it is impossible, that evil should thus triumph over good. I will not be submerged again. I have grown stronger as he has grown weaker and more wicked. He cannot hold out against me any longer. I shall give him one more chance to put his affairs in order and make it known that he will never return.

"It has been a hard-fought battle between us for the possession of this body. But I have won it. I am stronger than he is now and, if I wished, I could go out from this office and never let him see the light of day again. But it is right for him to have a few days more.

"And I want him to tell you one thing that he has done. He shall tell you with his own lips. It is your right to know, but he will not tell you the truth unless I make him. He shall come to see you tomorrow and you can try hypnotizing him if you want to. But before you begin give him an opportunity to make his confession. I shall make him speak. Goodnight, Dr. Annister."

The physician sat long in his big arm-chair, his forehead upon his locked fingers. When he arose his face was haggard and, unconscious of the movement, he pressed one hand against his breast.

"No," he said aloud, "I was right. There is a possibility that I can yet reincarnate these two warring principles of selfishness and altruism into one big-hearted, splendidly endowed human being. I must take the chances and do my best. Oh, man, man! How little you know what you are doing when you trifle with either your soul or your body! And what miracles you expect of us, to save you from the consequences you have richly earned—us who know so little more than you do!"

CHAPTER XXII

"A MOST INTERESTING CASE!"

Nine o'clock of the next evening came and passed. Dr. Annister dismissed his last patient, looked into his waiting room and found it empty, then sat down to wait for a few minutes, unwilling to take from Felix Brand what he feared might be his last chance.

"If I can give him some help tonight," the physician's thoughts ran, "if I can restore his self-confidence and his grip on himself, that will be just the impulse in the right direction that he needs. After that it will be easier for him and he may win yet. A most interesting case! More interesting even than Dr. Prince's Miss Beauchamp! The cleavage is complete and clean. If I can cure it, it will be the most remarkable case on record!"

There was a tap at the open door behind him and he heard Brand's voice saying, "Are you here, Dr. Annister?"

"Come in, Felix, come in," the doctor replied, rising, with more of professional interest than personal friendliness in his tones. "You've come for your first treatment, I suppose? Well, we'll see what we can do."

Brand was moving about the room with seemingly aimless steps, a curious unwillingness upon his face. Within himself he was feeling a sense of compulsion that was moving him against his will. Within his brain he seemed not so much to hear as to feel a voice saying, "Tell him! Tell him!" And with all his strength he was battling against these inward commands.

Dr. Annister noticed his stubborn look and the defiant poise of his head. "What is it, Felix?" queried the physician. "Don't you want to take the treatment? Have you changed your mind?"

"No, sir. I've not changed my mind. I'm more anxious than ever about it. Shall we begin at once?"

Suddenly his ears seemed to roar with the sound of "Tell him! Tell him! Tell him!" He started and glanced fearfully about the room.

"I will not! I will not! I will not!" His tongue formed the words of refusal behind closed lips, pressed together in a hard line.

Dr. Annister drew a quick, deep breath. "I'm not in very good shape tonight, Felix, but I'll do the best I can for you," he said, as he stepped to a cabinet at the back of the room, where he measured out and swallowed a dose of medicine. "Now, if you're ready, we'll begin," he went on, and was surprised to see his companion stagger back a step or two and pass his hand irresolutely over his face.

"Yes, Dr. Annister, at once. But there is something—" the words came slowly, in a monotonous, strained tone through his barely opened lips.

Sudden recollection flashed upon the doctor's mind of something Gordon had said the night before. He had forgotten it, in his interest in the peculiar features of the case, until that moment. "Oh," he exclaimed, "is there something you want to speak of first? What is it?"

Brand's face was pale, his eyes staring and his hands clenched in the struggle he was still making against that inward mastery bent on forcing him to a confession he was determined he would not make. For he greatly feared its effect upon Dr. Annister's intention to help him, while its other probable consequences he was most unwilling to accept.

But that other will within himself was stronger than his own determination. Already he felt his defiance growing numb before it. He walked irresolutely across the room and back while Dr. Annister looked at him with surprise and dawning suspicion.

"Well, what is it?" the physician repeated.

Felix stopped short and gave himself an angry shake. Then with a little snarl he faced about and began, with eyes averted:

"I don't suppose it will please you to hear it," he blurted out, and the other could not know that the sharpness in his tones was merely the expression of his futile rage against that hated other will, housed within his own body, that was forcing him to do a thing sure to interfere with his plans and pleasures. "But I'm going to tell you and you can make the best of it."

In his impotent anger he was ready now to say any ruthless thing that occurred to him. And not for any price would he have had Dr. Annister discover that he was not making this confession of his own accord.

"You said yesterday that the engagement between Mildred and me must be ended. Well, it is ended, but not in the way you meant. We are married."

"What! What do you say?" the doctor exclaimed, wheeling toward him with frowning brow.

"I said, we're married already. We've been married two months. I took her over to Jersey one day and we were married there."

"You dared—Felix Brand, you dared do this, knowing what you knew?"

"It seems so," the other coolly replied. "Mildred was quite willing," he went on with a little sneer. "I needed her love. I'd have been a fool not to take what she was ready to give me. And I married her. Maybe I was a fool to do that, but I did."

"A fool? You were a knave, a wretch, to take advantage of an innocent girl's love!" cried her father, moving toward him with threatening manner and blazing eyes. Then, suddenly, the physician staggered back and sank into his arm-chair.

"Leave me, Felix," he said, and though his tones were suddenly grown feeble, they still vibrated with angry contempt. "Go, now, at once. I don't want you near me. But I'll see you again about this matter. And if you try to communicate with Mildred I'll have you arrested! Go! Go!"

The architect turned on his heel and left the room. Dr. Annister sank wearily into his chair and his hands sought their accustomed position. Then they too fell back against his chest. "Mildred!" his white lips whispered, then stiffened and were still.

"Mildred!" His White Lips Whispered, Then Stiffened and Were Still

CHAPTER XXIII

WHITHER?

Felix Brand opened his eyes, then let the lids quickly flutter down again. He was afraid to look about him, for he was no longer sure where he might awaken after what seemed to him to have been no more than an ordinary night's sleep. Apprehensively he lifted one hand to his face and felt of his upper lip. There was no mustache upon it. Reassured, he opened his eyes again, and with deep relief gazed about his familiar bedroom.

"I guess it's still the next day after yesterday," he said to himself with profound satisfaction. For a moment he centered his attention upon himself. "And that damned Gordon has subsided," he muttered. "I don't feel him at all this morning. That's promising. I've had a good night's rest, now I'll have a good day and tonight I'll go to see Dr. Annister and let him begin—the devil!" Remembrance had flashed upon him of his last night's interview with the physician.

"But he promised to help me and he'll have to do it. I'll do anything he says about Mildred—let her divorce me if he wants her to. A wife's a nuisance. I'm sure I don't want to be tied up with one. What did I do it for anyway?"

Notwithstanding his confidence that there had been no hiatus in his life since his last waking hours, Brand glanced with some trepidation at the date line of the morning paper. "That's right," he thought.

His eyes dropped down over the headlines and he stopped stock still, his face paling. "Dead!" he exclaimed aloud. "Now what's to become of me!"

As he read the article, displayed prominently on the front page, which told of the death of Dr. Philip Annister, the famous nerve specialist, from heart-disease, he found that he had been, in all probability, the last person who had seen the physician alive. He remembered the sudden failure of strength which had sent the doctor staggering back into his arm-chair.

"I suppose," he said to himself, and was aware of no feeling of compunction, "it was what I told him that did the business. If that damned whelp Gordon had let me alone—what am I to do now?"

When the architect appeared at his office one look at him told Henrietta that she was not to have a comfortable day. "Well, it's my last one here," she thought, and had occasion, as the hours wore on, to repeat the assurance to herself many times, for comfort's sake. Doubly repellent though her service under him had become since that sad day of her sister's disaster, Henrietta had felt, nevertheless, that justice demanded of her to continue in it until the time for which she had given notice should expire. So, loyal to her sense of fairness, she had kept on, while aversion deepened into loathing and, of late, was even touched with fear.

Over and over again, as her troubles and apprehensions pressed sharply upon her, did her thoughts recur to Hugh Gordon with longing remembrance of the sense of protection and security she had felt in his presence. So much did she dwell upon her memories of the hours they had spent together that in her secret heart the feeling toward him of intimacy and confidence grew ever stronger, and more and more frequently the thought would leap into her mind, "I wish Hugh Gordon were here."

The day which was to be the last of her service as Felix Brand's secretary proved to be the most trying of all that she had endured. As one unpleasant episode succeeded another her eyes sought the clock again and again and she told herself, "It will be only four hours more," or, "Now it's only two hours and a half," and again, "In seventy minutes I shall be through."

As the hours dragged on it seemed to her that Brand's temper grew steadily worse. And he went restlessly from one thing to another, unable to concentrate his attention upon anything. He had on hand several pieces of work, all of which Henrietta knew he was anxious to finish as soon as possible. But he would take up first one, then another, only to throw each one down impatiently with a muttered oath after a few minutes of effort.

Henrietta did not know, as Dr. Annister had not known of his inward compulsion the night before, that within him a stern monitor was making its orders felt and trying to force him to write the message which was to set the seal of finality upon his next disappearance.

He was facing the utter annihilation of his soul, his personal being, while his body, dwelt in by his ruthless enemy, should still live on, seeing the sunshine, breathing the sweet air, loving life. He drew back, terrified but wrathful, from the brink of this black void to which his luring desires had led him.

What was it, that gulf of nothingness, into which his soul had plunged so many times already? Down, down, to what unplumbed depths had it gone, those other times? True, it had come back. But it had brought no tidings of that dumb, black vast into which it had sunk. And thinner and thinner had grown the thread that had drawn it back from that unsensed abyss until now he knew that it was ready to break. His soul was numb with the conviction that, let it be thrust once more over the brink, it would drop beyond recall into oblivion.

It was his own death warrant that this masterful force within him was ordering him to write—the death warrant of him, Felix Brand, ardent lover of life and but barely past its beginning, of all of him save only his fair physical envelope, which would still live and be glad, though he had passed into nothingness.

Stronger and stronger, the more he resisted, grew this inner compulsion, until it seemed to have entered into his every nerve and bone and muscle and he feared to remain at his desk lest it force his unwilling hand to write. For an hour he loitered about, staying his steps in other parts of the room, wherever he could make pretense of busying himself.

But at last, in the late afternoon, he suddenly found himself moving in the direction of his desk. He stopped, braced himself, took another step, another, and another, with feet that he could not compel to cling to the floor. And, after long minutes of struggle, he sank finally into his desk chair.

But even yet he would not give up. The muscles of his arm bulged, his neck sinews stood out and his eyes glared red and wrathful in the effort he was making to be his own master. But slowly, with jerking movements, impelled by that inexorable force, his hand moved across the desk, sought to stay itself upon book or inkwell, then, at last completely overmastered, took pen and wrote—wrote the words sent down to it by that dominating power that had taken possession of his will.

He glowered at the letter as it lay before him in its envelope, sealed, stamped and addressed to "Miss Mildred Annister," and muttered, "I'll not let it go! I'll tear it up! I'll get the best of him yet!"

At that moment his secretary appeared at his door and asked him concerning the disposition of certain papers. She was putting everything in order, she told him, so that her successor would have no difficulty in beginning the work.

"Can't you wait a minute?" he snarled at her over his shoulder.

"Oh, dear!" thought Henrietta, shrinking back. "What's wrong now, I wonder! Well, I'll be through in ten minutes, and nothing very dreadful can happen in that time."

Brand rose, swearing angrily, and turned upon her. The affright and consternation in her face maddened him the more.

"Well, what do you want?" he demanded roughly. She repeated what she had said.

"You're not going to quit today?" he exclaimed, striding back and forth, his heart raging against the letter on his desk and all that it meant.

She reminded him that the time for which she had agreed to remain expired that day. "Haven't you engaged any one else, Mr. Brand?" she asked, quailing a little as she saw the violent anger that possessed him.

"No! What time have I had to hunt up secretaries? I can't do without you. You'll have to stay another week."

Henrietta's spirit rose. "I shall not stay another day, Mr. Brand! I've given you ample notice, and I have secured another position. I go to work there next week."

He wheeled and strode toward her, a menacing figure. "I tell you, you'll have to stay another week! You'll get no more money from me unless you do!" he shouted.

She saw that he was beside himself with a rage that, to her, was inexplicable, and she retreated as he came onward until she stood with her back against the wall and he threatened in front of her, his face working with unrestrained passion. The thought flashed upon her that perhaps he had gone suddenly insane.

"You've got to stay," Brand shouted again. "I'll not pay you unless you do!"

He raised his clenched fist, as if he were about to strike her in the face. She threw up her arm to ward off the blow and her thoughts flew to the man upon whom they had dwelt so much these recent days, with quick longing for his care and protection.

"Oh, Hugh! Hugh! If you were here!" she whispered.

Low as was the sound it reached the ears of him who stood in front of her with drawn fist and threatening mien. He started back and she, with her arm before her face, did not see the awesome look that leaped across his countenance. His arm dropped and for a moment his face was the battle-ground of fierce, contending wills and furious passions. Then his whole body writhed as if in a convulsion, his arms sprang straight up in the air and a cry of mortal agony, of defeat, despair and hopeless, futile wrath rang through the room.

So uncanny and so heartbroken was that cry, as might be the howl of a lost soul raging impotently, that it seemed to stop the course of the very blood in her veins. In fear and terror she dropped her guarding arm, half feeling already the blow she expected to receive in her face, and quailing from the raving madman she was sure was about to spring upon her.

But instead of Felix Brand, frenzied and brutal, her eyes fell upon the man whose help she had invoked. Hugh Gordon was before her, his arms upraised as if in gratitude to heaven, his lifted face glowing with triumph. She stared at him with wide, terrified eyes and cowered against the wall, all her faculties numbed by the awesomeness of this miraculous thing.

"I've won!" Gordon was crying in exultant tones. "That beast is conquered at last, for good and all!"

He strode a few paces up the room and back, and his figure seemed to grow before Henrietta's very eyes in his exultation over his victory. As he turned back his gaze fell upon the terrified girl at whose need he had sprung, with mighty effort, into final, lasting dominance.

"Don't be frightened," he said gently, leaning toward her with outstretched, reassuring hand. "You called me, and I came—came to help you, to save you, and to love you. You have nothing to fear now. That incarnate baseness has sunk down, down, too deep for resurrection! He shall never return!"

"Hugh! Hugh!" she quavered. "What have you done with him? Where is he?"

Upon Gordon's exultant countenance there fell a shade of solemnity. "I know not," he replied in awed tones. "What has become of him is one of the mysteries of the human soul, a mystery whose beginning and whose growth I understand, as you shall too, but whose end no man can explain. The man whom you knew, whom everyone knew, who knew himself, as Felix Brand, is no more. He will never exist again.

"Deliberately that man chose the worse side of his nature and cherished it and tried to ignore and cast out the other, the better side. But, deep down within him, that other side lived and grew strong, until it was strong enough to take possession of his body and cast him out. He is gone!" Gordon's voice rose again into triumphal tones. "He has dropped into an oblivion man's thought cannot fathom nor man's brain understand. He ordained his own destiny, he worked out his own fate. Let him have the end that he himself invited!"

Gordon ceased speaking and leaned toward Henrietta. The terror had left her countenance and in her eyes was the dawning of renewed trust in him.

"Come," he said, "let us leave this place, with all of its wretched memories."

And he took her hand and led her forth.

THE END.

Lightning Source UK Ltd.
Milton Keynes UK
UKHW040948291119
354426UK00001BA/29/P